THE
HELL BENT
KID

THE
HELL BENT
KID

A Novel

CHARLES O. LOCKE

OPEN ROAD

INTEGRATED MEDIA

NEW YORK

Cover design by Drew Padrutt

ISBN: 978-1-5040-5332-7

This edition published in 2018 by Open Road Integrated Media, Inc.
180 Maiden Lane
New York, NY 10038
www.openroadmedia.com

THE
HELL BENT
KID

-1-

STATEMENT BY HENRY RESTOW

After the first Indian fighting quieted down, and the hard-pan camps and towns moved west, killings were less common in north-west Texas than people were led to think. So my ranch got a name for itself when the Kid was with us. "They've got a murderer penned up over at the Restow place" was the way people put it.

This Kid—Tot Lohman—was no murderer and was not penned up. He knew he had to stay on the place, the way I had fixed it with the sheriff. Also, he had killed Shorty Boyd in self-defense, although I think he made a mistake in not saying how it was done. The Boyds said Shorty had been shot. Lohman let it go that way. There was supposed to be more honor to it, if it involved a bullet. On both sides.

When Tot Lohman was probated to me, he had one thing on his mind. His family had been pretty well wiped out, except one brother and his father, who suddenly took consumption and seemed to be dying a slow death. The father, who had been a fine peace officer, pulled up stakes and went into the territory of New Mexico, looking like a skeleton that walked and leaving his son in Texas, which led to the shooting, if it was a shooting, that landed the boy on me.

Lohman wanted to follow his father bad. He wanted to help his father. The father never revealed just what he wanted. He had become sick and vague on most things.

When I hired Lohman I offered him eight dollars a month as a ranch hand. The grown hands got eleven. Lohman held out, saying he could do a man's work and when I agreed on full pay, he immediately cut it back to nine to pay me for my favor to him with the law—the difference in pay he meant, this would pay me off. This seems strange but it was like Lohman. He wanted to be thought of as a man but he wanted to pay his way in everything. He even tried to pay me for some cast-off clothes which he needed badly. Also, three times I arranged for him to send small sums of money to his father. He had managed to save these out of his earnings.

At the time Lohman came to me he gave his age as 18. He was between 10 and 11 above five feet, I would say, thin but well-muscled, with brown hair and peculiar, dark, blue eyes. He was a fair worker with cattle. Only fair. But he was good with horses because he liked them almost as well as guns. He was the best shot with a rifle I have ever seen, and I doubt if a greater natural genius with a rifle ever lived in these parts. I have never seen Lohman dangerous, but imagine he could be very dangerous with a rifle, if sufficiently aroused.

One other qualification Lohman had was his ability to write a good hand, something his mother had taught him. Also from some early training he had started to keep a sort of diary and continued *to do so, which I am told requires a good deal of character in the individual.*

My daughter on her two visits said of him: "He is too young to have that shadow on his face."

-2-

NARRATIVE BY LOHMAN

When I first agreed to stay at the Restow place after I had killed Shorty Boyd, it seemed the sensible thing to do. I had planned before the killing to work for Restow. Now that I was probated to him, he was willing to hire me.

My father had gone into Mexico, and it was thought I would some day go down there and join him. But not hearing from my father worried me. Also, while I wanted no trouble with the Boyds, it got said around that I was hiding from them on the Restow ranch. Also, I began to see a change in the attitude of the hands, and in Marcus, the foreman.

Marcus had never seemed to like me from the start, due to nothing but natural dislike. I also felt this way. But I was always civil and obedient to him.

I spoke to him on a certain day about seeing Mr. Restow and he passed the word. Restow passed the word back by the cook who cooked for both the big house and the outfit that when I saw the shade up in the big room I should go in.

Sat on the fence after dinner and waited. About one the shade went up and I went in. This time I made it strong to Mr. Restow about getting off the ranch and down to my father in the territory.

Mr. Restow had some letters to write, but said that he and Marcus and I would talk about it that night.

He said he thought Marcus's advice would be good for both of us, Marcus knowing something of the New Mexico territory. I doubted Marcus's attitude to me would be fair, but agreed.

Almost immediately after this something happened that could have changed my mind, if I had felt it had changed Marcus.

When I went back to my corral work we were having a cap of rain. I saw Marcus at the shed end near the chutes. He was leaning over pouring grain from a grainsack to a nosebag. Both his horse and a little burro-colored horse I owned were loose-hobbled halfway up the slope behind the corral. But inside the fence was a mean little mustang horse named Pancho. This horse we had all teased a little and Marcus had spur-marked. He was coming up from behind before I could yell.

That little horse took Marcus's slicker collar in his teeth and shook him as a dog will a rat. Then he began to rear and strike with new-shod forefeet, and drawing blood.

The next time the mustang reared, pulling Marcus well off the ground, I threw a wheel wrench under him hitting his testicles square. He yelled and dropped Marcus.

After we got Marcus in his bunk, Mr. Restow wanted to get a doctor from Marshall, but Marcus bucked. He was proud of his physical strength, and insisted we go right ahead and talk that night, as planned. So while the rest played blackjack, and one hand played The Dove softly on the mouth organ, Mr. Restow and I sat beside Marcus's bed, which was the only one in the bunkhouse, the rest bunks.

Marcus started to roll a cigaret, botched it and dropped tobacco all over the blanket, and rolled another. Mr. Restow tapped the floor with one of his 100 dollar Juarez boots.

"I say let the boy go to his father," said Marcus. "His father needs him. He is getting to be no good around here. His father is in trouble. He wants to join in and help him. That's natural."

Restow said: "I'm willing to let him leave the ranch but I want him to head east. Tot's father is old enough to take care of himself. If Tot goes west and south he will surely meet the Boyds and get killed."

"Pretty good with a rifle," said Marcus.

Restow said nothing.

Marcus got his cigaret going. "You'll never get the boy to stay here." He frowned at me. I think his dislike of me had been somewhat cured by my act that afternoon. But it was hard to tell about Marcus. He had been made bitter by Comanches disfiguring his mouth with rawhide when a child. He had a perpetual smile, but not a cheerful one. You could never tell whether he was pleased or angry even with himself, such as after his champion rope work, using the biggest wire-plaited honda I ever saw.

But he turned on me sharp: "All right, let's chase it out in the clear. You got some gossip from that freighter down at the Silver Spur. Well, the same thing came to me. I understand your father is mixed up with lawless men and threatened with jail. He must be light-headed. He seems to need a guardian. But I don't think you qualify. It takes an older man."

Mr. Restow said: "I can explain this being mixed up with lawless men. Tot's father is cooking for this Englishman's outfit. The outfit is having some trouble with cattle inspectors. The country is still rough down there. All kinds of people are moving in and out of Socorro and places. There are cattle-lifters, of course, but ranchers are also stealing from each other. I ought to know as I have something of a stake down there. Lohman is cooking because he's not fit for heavy work. It don't make sense Lohman would one day be a peace officer up here, with his fine record, and the next day turn into a cattle thief."

"Funny things happen," Marcus said.

Restow was getting angry now, and Marcus saw this and said: "Why not let the kid speak his piece?"

So then I did. I told them I knew more than they gave me credit for. I told them I knew the two younger Boyds were back from the east after being sent to school there or for a trip. That it was well known Old Man Boyd would not hold them down. That it was only a matter of time till I would get shot or shot at on or off the ranch. I told them I wanted to get to my father bad and was determined to ride west and south and not east just for safety.

I then played my strongest card, which was that Restow was now president of the Peaceable Committee of North Texas made up to keep peace, and that if I got shot on his ranch, it might be embarrassing.

Restow opened his eyes wide at this. Marcus laughed right out. Till the day I die I will never know whether Marcus wanted me to go or stay. But I would think he wanted me to go.

They asked me would I take the stage and I said no. I would have to change twice and then maybe not make it. Mr. Restow wanted to give me a horse. I said I had my own and he said, "If you mean that little mouse-colored pony with the set-fast back sore you had better let me give you a real horse." But I said no I was used to Jimmy.

We got up from our chairs then and Restow went ahead while I followed him outside. He asked me about guns and I said I had my rifle, and about clothes and I said I had enough, and about money, and I showed him how I carried the dollars I had, each silver dollar under a little sewed patch inside my waistband, so I could get a dollar by knifing a thread loose.

He said goodbye, and expressed regret. He handed me a letter he had written to a friend in the territory.

I had won my argument without telling what was the most in my thinking. I had heard so much about the Boyds since Shorty's death that I was getting a feeling that we should meet and get it over with.

That night I did not sleep well. I kept thinking about the trip, but also my mind kept going back to the past. I had been the home boy of my family. I was with my mother a lot till she died, because she needed me, and what she told me stayed with me a long time. This all took place while two of my brothers were growing up, getting to be peace officers and getting killed fast. My mother taught me to read and write and counseled me good.

My mind kept going back to the times when on fair days my mother would take me out on the flat under some trees where the only sound except her reading was the wind and the rustle. She had a mouth like a girl. I used to watch her lips forming the words. She read slowly and carefully and then would stop and explain. She was a Quaker woman, my mother was.

Womenkind have soft ways and I think my mother prevented me from hardening up like my brothers. But after she died, I toughened up fast. My father taught me to shoot. But you don't have to be hard to shoot. In fact in some ways it helps to be soft when shooting—and careful. To be easy. To use your mind.

LOHMAN STARTS HIS TRIP

Marcus and I were up before anyone the next morning. I fried some beans for myself and shared coffee with Marcus. He was on his big black in the yard when I got on my horse. He sat there looking at me. He had on a clean shirt and a Sunday hat.

Mr. Restow had insisted he must ride to Toscoso or Twist to see a doctor about his back. If he went to Toscoso, he would also see his girl, a prostitute.

Marcus said: "You better keep your mouth buttoned over in the territory. There is also good shots over there. I would advise you to get into Socorro below the Panhandle across the Grande, but down there you might get yourself Pecosed."

I agreed.

"If," said Marcus, "you figure on coming back here for your job, forget it. You can't work for me again. You are big-balled for a shoat."

I was about to say it was my understanding Restow did the hiring and firing, but Marcus had started off.

The road I was to take forked off north about a mile west of the Restow place. Marcus could have taken the South Fork after riding the mile with me. But he paralleled for half a mile, and then threw a pistol shot at me. A cut of dust showed in front of my pony, stopping him.

Sometimes a cowpoker will shoot wild at another to attract his attention, or for fun. So I took it easy. But when a second shot was laid over the first, I out with the rifle from the scabbard and shot three times at Marcus.

Marcus wiggled his fingers at me and laughed. I could see him laughing with his head back, as he ran his horse off behind a pitch of land. What worried me was not his shooting at me for meanness. It was my rifle had jammed after the third shot. It made me wish I again had the Spencer that had been stolen from me.

As I went on with the Staked Plains on my right, and later when I was forced into the edge of them, I kept thinking about this, worrying about it. Noon my eyes at a pool where I drank looked like holes in a pan of dust. The heat and dust were terrible and I wasn't used to them. The Restow ranch had softened me up.

I put miles behind me that day, pressing Jimmy hard. That night I slept out near a small half-dry creek, but near people, because just before bedding down I stopped at a Mex woman's place. She was out in front of her little dobe shack drying washed grain, with strings of chili behind her, so I asked for some little bite.

A little girl came out of the place then. There was a tortilla laid flat on her hand with gravied beans on it. She was dragging her right leg that was wizened away. I got a few drinks from their well which took care of quite a neighborhood, and made the little girl a cornhusk doll like I had made for my sister Julia.

Next morning the day was fine, but hot from early hours on. After a good start, the sun got even hotter. I moved north to the dryer ground of the North Stakes. I got some longer and dryer miles behind me that day and made really good time.

At a little water place with a grab of box elder I slept and started off again. The sun heated up but the view was wonderful. The high plains were flat here, except for the low hills and midget buttes to the north. Smells got sharp, the heat baking out the oil from the saddle skirts that I had oiled heavy because of their age.

The wind blew the green-smelling suds back from Jimmy's mouth. At sundown Jimmy was heaving. He worried the bit between heaves so I took off the bridle and rode him with the hackamore. Then walk and lead him awhile.

That Jimmy was a willing pony, even half sick. He had had too much green feed without being used to it. He was almost a pet horse, and would shake hands.

When I stopped I cleaned my rifle. On the go, I had worried about the sun baking the oil out of her, so in the saddle I had slapped on a finger full of bacon grease. Now I removed this because of the salt.

I had remembered a water hole and some box elders I was now headed for. They were there all right, but the creek was dry as dead skin, except for a small pool going down fast I had one water can, no canteen, so I went easy.

With Jimmy hobbled, I ate raw stuff and heated some coffee which I have never liked. I was tired and jumpy, knowing I was in the Boyd country.

After my last trip for water, I saw the biggest rattler I ever saw, sliding down to drink there. He saw me but paid me no mind of course. He looked half sick and something was wrong with one of his eyes, like scaling over. His smell was bad and when I saw where he came from, an old gopher hole, I moved up there and the smell would of sickened a coyote.

So I moved around but when the slack wind moved around with me the smell came with it. So I picked a little kind of half-dust hogback-and-rock and got down behind her, poor cover against smell or anything.

Wrapped up, I watched the stars in the sky. Jimmy seemed to eat all night. All night I could hear him clanking his hobble iron and chewing. What on, I wondered. Also I tried to sleep without success. My mind kept wandering to the Boyds, and also went over the past events of my life.

I remembered the day the Comanches raided our farm to get horses and how my father was away and I was there with my older brothers, I being 12. I remembered how we got the horses into the barn, but my baby sister Julia was arrow-shot coming back from the creek with a small fish one of us had caught and left there. And how my mother came out on the doorstep and called to Harley, who was always slow, and Nevin picked up the baby, turning his back to my mother and hacking off the shaft with his knife.

And I recalled how my mother sat on the doorstep holding Julia the rest of the day long after the Indians had gone with only one horse of ours, not moving nor speaking to anyone.

Then I went back over the poetry books she had read me out under a tree, and the deep-cold winter when she died, with a wet, beautiful spring afterward, the sky like a big blue glass dome all the way from Cap Rock to the Llano Estacado.

◆ ◆ ◆

When the first light came, I got up shaky and sleepy, just in time to see the ridge of higher ground not standing but flowing northeast to southwest. Then I saw it was a rattler, maybe a new one or the same one, going down to drink. He crawled on the profile, making the land seem to move. I decided I had picked a snaky place.

Took a little water for coffee, figuring on a late start because of poor sleep. Still there was half light with the light coming slowly, as if rain was due.

My doughball was in the spider and I threw a strip of bacon after it. It was a poor fire of a few yucca stems, grass and trash.

I felt of the spider and it was only warm, with wind blowing the yellow fire from under it and coals not formed yet. So I sat down to wait with my back to the little rise of ground, pushing my coffee pot nearer. Still I could not come fully awake.

I watched Jimmy for a minute, worrying his nose among grass and stems, off back from the rise. Then I believe I dozed off, woke up with a jump. I must have slept a half hour. The pot was blacked up, fire near out and the stuff in the skillet sad-greasy.

The ground rumbled behind me. Then I heard a bawl, then saw about four or five strays off to the north, rose up, whirled and saw the Boyds.

The Boyds were on in advance, and behind them was about three, four hundred cattle, like ghost cattle, because even then they was a good piece off. They were drifting easy, coming on me like rain gathering and approaching. The wind was fairly loud, with long quiet spells, and dust heavy over to the west.

The wing riders were two other men, one I judged to be a Boyd, a little to the rear. I counted about five men, and I suppose they might have had a sixth, a clean-up man pushing the bunch easy from behind. They must have been night-moving that herd for water or have gotten a very early start.

I got hold of my rifle and as I picked her up was glad to know how carefully I had cleaned her the night before. I let her hang loose in my right hand, using my thumb to set back the hammer ready to work the first shot fast. I had never seen such strong odds.

On my right Tom was fast in coming up. I knew him right away for he was the dudy one of the two, with tapaderos that almost touched the ground. He was swinging his trick pony hard so that his pockets scooped dust as they say, and I remembered his wavy, yellow hair and his fast, long legs and smile at the schoolhouse dance where he was all shirted up in white with new, store pants, and his fast stepping feet that charmed the girls.

Then Otis came up on the left much slower and remembered him, too, at the schoolhouse dance where I had killed Shorty Boyd, his quiet manner and his thin, kind looking face that fooled you and his dry, sharp way of talking.

But now both the Boyds looked as I had seen myself—eyes like holes in a pan of dust. They must have had a hard night and hard times before that gathering the ruckus of steers out of the hills and shaping them up and getting them started. With that many men I knew they were after more strays and long on the move since then for the hills were miles off.

Tom put his hand to his mouth and yelled to Otis—"You see what I see?"

Otis moved up a little on his mare—unusual to be riding. She was crossing her forefeet among stones in a dainty way as she slow-walked. I saw both their hands move and with the wind lulling I could even hear a cylinder click. They had possibly been turning a stray or so with a pistol shot that morning or had run into a prairie dog town with plenty of snakes, so by hand and feel they were throwing the live shell one-away.

I raised my muzzle a little.

In the quiet that seemed to come it was plain when Tom said: "Watch it. He's a sneak-shot."

Otis said: "I'm watching it."

I stood there. The Boyds did not move but the cattle did. They came on slow. In the light, changing wind and the dust drift they were like a dream. With dust ghosts behind and above them, blowing and nodding and then sloping down fast so they hid part of the mass out of which a bawl now and then would come, they now smelt water clear. Tom's horse moved a little and he slapped his morale down hard like a shot and the horse jumped a little. One old poker I recognized began to gallop in and out of the herd at edges, but Otis called him and he came up behind. I got the thought then that there were no calfs nor mothers in the mill, with here and there a bloody crest showing the bulls had been fighting. And those steers needed water bad, had been hard driven all night, and had possibly the jumps and were unsluggish having been light fed in dry canyons for weeks.

As both Boyds started letting me have it, yelling above the shots as if to put poison in the slugs, I ducked down, then whirled once when one of Otis's came too close and felt the crease and the shock of something behind the crease wound back of my right thigh. But I concentrated on the herd leaders, and carefully shot high on, and my shots took the right effect, for I could see the chips fly from the horns of one baldy.

They started, slowed and almost stopped as if to get ready for the real rush. If they had come on square at me, I would have been a blood spot and the Boyds would have died in seconds. As it was, the herd started, slowed, then turned a quarter with the long ground slope in front of them where I stood. The brothers were the most surprised men I ever saw.

They were busy getting turned, trying to give their mounts a chance to balance against the rush. The steers rampaged off to the right. First I saw Otis and his horse lifted up, then dropped, then lifted again. I heard him scream among the howl and drum of the steers. Then I saw the steers climbing Otis and his horse, and he was out of sight somewhere under his horse and among the dust. I saw his horse killed. Tom had been quicker and was out of the way.

With the men and the horses and steers mingling and the ground near shaking with the rush, and the dust rising, a strange thing happened. This was that a red scut of blood like a hell-red rainbow came up from the center, shooting to the sky, then bending over and fanning away south. Some horn had slashed a big artery in a cow or horse. Times later I told a Mex about it, and he rolled his eyes and said it was the Whip of God. Said he had seen similar. It is possible he had.

The way Otis screamed at first, then a low whimpering, while the steers angled off from me to my right in the natural dip of the land had me paralyzed. Then the red mess they made of Otis's horse. For there was so many cows pronged on her with others behind coming fast that the mare was lifted up and rolled back, being ripped to pieces on top of the heads and horns. It was very unusual for Otis to be riding that little mare. I pitied her. I was sorry for all. This was more than I had figured.

I stood there watching. Tom Boyd seemed to double back and then go on. He was trying to turn the cows toward the higher bushed places to brake them. But his double-back had been for Otis, and to yell to the others to help. They came and pulled Otis from under his dead horse, what was left, and a dead cow. Otis was in bad shape, looking half dead.

They first set him on another horse without paying me mind, but then he slumped and they laid him across his stomach and a cowhand, coming from back, led him south toward their remuda. Tom turned and stared at me. I saw him fooling with his gun, but he did nothing with it. He looked at me and I think he called me every name I had ever heard. Then he started talking low to the men. They were talking, looking at me, then looking at what I first thought was an old tarp or wagon cover lying near Otis's horse. Then I saw it was the old hand I knew who would never jab cattle again. I thought to myself, yes, the Boyds started it, and Otis may be hurt but if somebody is killed it would not be one of the Boyds, oh no.

They left the man right there. I thought they were going to rush me for a while, but then all rode off. I still waited. Sure enough back soon came what I supposed was their best shot, a middle-age Mex who had grown up on the Boyd place. He got behind a rock and began to throw at me with a hard-hitting carbine. I took cover, but was not too careful, as he must have been excited, had probably been scolded too much.

This went on for about an hour. I just let him shoot. His trigger finger must have gotten tired. But then I got tired, for it got to be considerable strain. I had hardly shot, so he got careless. When he crawled for a high spot under fair cover I caught him in the elbow and must have damaged him badly. He shot a few more times, then got on his horse and rode off fast, holding his right arm tight against him.

I wondered what Old Man Boyd would say to his sons about the spooked herd.

-4-

LOHMAN STARTS ACROSS
THE DRY

When I turned around I knew how much they must have hated me in the way they had shot Jimmy. Of course, it might have been a mistake. But I don't think it was. And who shoots a man's horse?

Jimmy was still alive, but he kept trying to raise up on his forelegs and then he would flop back. The wound was deep in his back just even with the sheath. At my first thought of water to ease him, I looked at the water hole. The unherded cows had not touched too much of it. Two were still standing looking at it and I scared them off with their tails up.

Trying to make up my mind about Jimmy, I began to wonder when the Boyds would be back. On the ground was the crumped-up body of the old cowhand, and I walked over to him and turned away and back. Much of him had been mashed flat.

Now the herd was like a dust cloud and I figured that all would have their hands too full for a while to bother about me. Also so much hand gun shooting made men careless about a rifle and that and its range and accuracy always gave me something of an advantage. They knew that. But then the thought rose up— would they be back at all? Did they need to come back, and did they have that figured? I knew the waterless miles behind me, and possibly the same before. And no horse. Was that why they killed him or tried to, that is? I knew I would have to kill him.

I began to get fairly scared.

I looked at Jimmy. I did not want to waste a shell. Decided I had better let him go out slowly. But when I got my knife and kneeled down beside him to open a neck artery, he threw his head over my knee, looking at me, so I gave up. Moving back then, I shot him with the rifle.

I looked at the hills and the low rising ground to the north. The hills looked small and low. Near as they might look to one who wanted to get there, they were probably three times as far.

My limited size can was a thick pool at the bottom, after draining out for the morning coffee. Cleaning it with grass and sand as well as I could, I filled it, and then did bleed Jimmy after all, taking about a quart from his neck in a tin bottle that once had oil in it. This would possibly be for both food and drink.

I hated to leave the saddle, so I packed it which was foolish, but cut the two saddle bags in half, carrying one, leaving the other.

In the one bag I put the little food I had and few little things and took my rifle. What I left with Jimmy was a lot—his grain sack, half full, box of small spare rifle parts, some clothes, tent half, rope bridle and hackamore, and heavier cooking stuff. Of course, I took the spider along with the water can.

Seemed good sense to head north toward the hills. Behind me I knew it was dry for miles. Before me the land got greener and water seemed likelier. Also, I hated to turn back. There was a good chance of getting to the Cimarron by second or third night, but I hoped to hit water before.

I started and did pretty good till noon. But my mouth got dry, even with wetting now and then from the can. After a noon rest, I started again. It was maybe two or three to judge by the shadows. The high plains was mostly grass but dry. A lot had been grazed off or pounded down, so bare stretches were frequent.

Just about night I looked at the hills. They seemed not much nearer. About seven when I bedded down, figuring on a big sleep to prepare for what was to come, luck was with me. There was a knob of rock stuff near and a pool with a handful or two of water in it. I dug around thinking it might be a plugged spring. This was not likely, seeing it was a plains pool, though with high ground near. It had some shade and proved to be just a rain left-over. I recalled I had seen distant rain in the morning.

The blood I sipped at and did not try again. Too much salt and the following effects did not seem good. So I poured out the blood and half filled the bottle. I had two fair drinks from the pool besides. The water situation now could have been worse.

Middling was how I felt the next morning. First thing, as usual, I looked well around me for the Boyds. No sign of Boyds but later I saw some distant riders to the south and tried to flag them down. I was chancing they were Boyds, but hoping they were not. They paid me no mind. Ate no breakfast, knowing that would build a thirst.

I walked that day and well into the night. The hills got some nearer. In the next morning, it was hard for me to move, but when I stood up, I got down again quick behind my grab of bush. A big party of Indians was moving slantwise across my trail about a mile and a half on ahead. They had no baggage nor squaws with them and were moving fairly fast.

It was plain what they had in mind. But they eased my fears about the Boyds returning. Besides knowing what I knew of Old Man Boyd—that he would trim down his sons for what I did to them and keep their minds occupied—I knew that now the Boyds would have other matters to think about.

If these were Comanches I was watching, and I thought they were, they were looking for two things. That is, two things besides trouble. They wanted horses and cattle, and it would almost have to be Boyd cattle.

Walked that day and well into the night. The hills got some nearer. In the morning, again it was hard for me to move. I looked at the can. What was inside did not look like water. But I got it down. My throat seemed pretty badly swole. I thought of my bacon slab, or even a dab of cooking grease I had left. I tossed the idea around quite a while because I was so hungry— Chew a section of fat for wetness. Then go crazy with the salty dryness. I finally decided against it.

The hills, when the day got clear, seemed about forty miles off. I had to leave my saddle. Went ahead, hauling one bag.

When I walked I got the fantods and saw Julia, my baby sister, the day she was arrow-shot. She was very clear to me and stayed a long time. Then I could see Shorty Boyd lying dead. I recalled how the whole thing started—with a glass of water I got for his girl. At her request.

The water thoughts pushed everything else out of my mind, and I saw many filled glasses, and saw the ocean waves, too, which I had only seen in pictures.

While stopping to rest, which I did a good deal of now, I began to notice my crease wound in the back of my thigh. When the sitdowns became more frequent I began to notice it more. I tried sitting on anything that came up from the surface of the ground with just one side of my rear.

I started up again once after a long rest and saw new visions. Saw a tank wagon roll by with water dripping, and then a chuck wagon with a water barrel on behind, then a Mex riding with a skin full of wine on his horse.

I looked at the slopes when my mind cleared and they and the jackpines were miles off. I followed a dry then, as it curved along, and found a puddle as big as a hoof mark. Lying down, it was hard to get at it with my mouth, but I think I got it with my tongue, if it was really there. Then I saw another and knew after investigating it was a mistake.

Slept then and woke up cursing some, though I have never been a great hand to curse. But in my dream and later on my thinking I began to see how it was. I began to see there is a system in the world, and that people like the Boyds have it fixed for you and keep it fixed. If you have something worthwhile they will take it from you, for I had heard the Boyds early worked that way when the country was new. But if you have nothing worthwhile they will take even that, if they are a mind to.

Because, I kept telling myself, they took my freedom first because Shorty Boyd got what he was asking from me, as everybody in their right mind said. Second they took whatever good name I might have had. Third, they took my horse by killing him. Fourth,—

I could not think of Fourth because I was thickheaded. But when my mind got cleared and back on the track, I nearly found it. The fourth thing had not been taken yet, but would be possibly. Yes, the Boyds would take this Fourth thing.

This is how I figured it. I said to myself I have nothing but these old clothes and this rifle. I knew they didn't want those. So the Fourth thing is my life. They want that.

I got to wondering then if I had figured it wrong. I thought it might be simpler. That it was just a case of the Boyds taking anything that struck them worth taking. Now I had it. The Boyds were born takers. They were born to take from people who softly give.

In my slow thinking I tried to remember something my father once told me about the way humans act. I tried to link this up with my thinking about the Boyds. I gave up. I told myself that if I got out of this, I would have long miles to think and hook up thoughts from here to Socorro. I fell asleep and dreamed and woke up shaking.

I had dreamed over something that happened to me when my father took me to town years before. He had gone to a saloon to arrest a man and had left me in a harness shop. The Ketcham outfit took over the shop in cross-street fighting with the Grey Brothers who owned the Lazy H. Behind a barrel used for soaking leather I could see the street and the fracas. I saw two of the Grey outfit killed when they tried to run from a grocery to a saloon.

Upstairs of the saloon was a dead prostitute. She had been shot trying to move from one window to the other over the porch roof. Her body was caught in the window. All you could see was her bustle shape. She was kneeling there half through the window with her back to us.

The way the Ketcham men talked between shots at the Greys when they would throw a shot at her and the way her rear jumped when the slugs hit and what they said sickened me. I had never heard women talked about that way.

When my father came for me, I became sick. He thought it was fright. I never told him it was the way the men talked about that dead girl. I wanted to kill them. I had never known what kind of men was loose in north Texas.

Later I wished to tell my mother at home of this matter on my mind. But I did not wish to pain her, so said nothing.

When you are down, going through difficult times, dreams hit you like this one. Gradually, I got rid of the horrors but they left a smell.

In the long afternoon the shadows from rocks seemed to reach for me. I knew I had to make a few more miles that day but wanted to lie down and sleep. I got started in a while and forced myself.

LOHMAN NEAR HIS FINISH

At noon I started right out. But after a hundred yards the sun knocked me down. I must have laid there a long time.

I had one dream right after the other now. I was waking between, trying to get up, then sleeping. So finally I slept right into the night. I had tried some walking by night and sleeping by day, but there was no day-cover to sleep under.

Next day I saw some far-off riders, took off my shirt and tried to wave them down. But they didn't see me or seem to. I saw no Boyds but hit plenty of water holes their herds had used up. I crossed plenty cow and pony tracks and some dry arroyos that meant hope. I found one small pool that was so bad I could hardly get the stuff down. It was scum-thick with small things moving slow in it.

My hands were getting sore as well as my face. I could almost see my hands dry-frying.

One place further along I picked up a couple of Comanche arrows and a little water gourd—empty. Later I picked up a head-cloth from a young brave.

Thinking of wet things, I got to thinking about a little bottle of horse linimint I used for Jimmy's back. I got scared fearing I would drink some. I clawed it out of the bag and threw it as far as I could, seeing the cork come out, seeing it turn over and over spraying yellow stuff in circles. Then I regretted I threw it. Then I knew how smart I had been to throw it.

Now I was walking slower, finding it helped to count the steps. The dance of the hills began—near, far, near, far. I saw I was walking slow and discovered I was crawling. I was on my hands and knees in the dusty grass pushing along.

Now that I was crawling, I saw that if I covered my hands and the back of my neck with dust, they would get less burn. I was angry I had not thought of that before. My hands were so bad they had small holes starting on their backs.

I began to feel like a gopher, pushing along, covering myself with dust. Trying to crawl and dig in at the same time weakened me both physically and mentally, and I finally realized I was a goner. So I just lay there and waited for it.

It is probable I slept a long time. When I woke up I could feel something inside me, pushing me blindly without my will taking part. I began to measure the crawl by inches and the resting by seconds that I tried to count.

When something moved ahead of me, I thought it was a snake, though nothing like snakes or gilas would have meant much to me then. But it was not a snake but a sick baby jack looking at me. It hardly moved when I reached out and grabbed it.

I had gotten so weak I could hardly get out the knife to slit its neck quick and easy. Botched it, but it died right off. But then when I held it over my face, lying on my back, I could not get any blood in my mouth, my lips and tongue were that swole. I tried a few times. Finally, I had to be satisfied with the blood falling on my face, moisturing me a little. But the blood-salt made my cracked face and mouth burn.

It may have been just as well. The jack might have been snake-bit. In my weakened state it might of finished me. And yet it might not of been that way at all. There are more differing ideas about snake poison than there are snakes.

When I started crawling again, I began to notice how my rifle was slowing me, slung on my back. So now I unlooped the sling and found a little piece of rope in one pocket and with the sling and rope like a drag rope I began dragging the rifle along two yards behind tied to my middle.

Mostly I crawled through grass that I was always hoping would be wet and cool but was dry. In the grassed-off places I would slow up to keep the dust quiet so as not to choke me.

Toward the finish I could make only inches at a time. My ears got to roaring. The pain of my stomach sometimes rose up over the pain of my backside wound. Suddenly it seemed to me my legs were paralyzed.

Not able to bend my knees, I began pulling myself along by the grass roots and yucca stems. I may have been moving at this time, or fooling myself. Believe I moved a little.

The pain of the sun and the pain of the sores all blotted out in a general feeling of dryness and suffocation, which was just as well for me. I could stand that better and also it seemed my body got lighter to drag along.

This, I figured, was not surprising as the water had all been baked out of me. I began to learn a great deal about grass roots and such and the small things that live in dry places—spiders, beetles and little small things like river crabs. I had never known they were there in such amounts. They kept my mind busy in the rest places.

I believe I slept a long time the last day till towards night, then started crawling again, feeling my stomach scrape, but finding I could use my legs again. I heard a noise and listened carefully to be sure. It first sounded like water and I began to make noises in my throat that I had planned as yells.

I listened again and was sure it was not water. It was some other sound I was not acquainted with. Then I thought I knew and began to try yelling again without success. It sounded like wind in trees.

I crawled ahead and began to feel rocky ground. Then rising ground. Then more rocks. Then when my hand touched certain things I began to make grunting noises like a pig which I had planned as yells. Because what I touched I was sure was pine needles.

Still I could not see. I lay there and then started crawling straight up, blind as I was. But then I eased to the right, knowing I must go around the slope, not up, or I might parallel water all the way to the top. I had to go faster. I was powered to do this, by the feeling of hope inside. So then I made a big hitch in my strength and got on my feet and made better time, jerking the rifle loose from the knots and the drag, for I could now use my rifle for a cane. I must of heard water fifteen times. I found it was always a trick of sound.

But after a long time I seemed to hear water right at my elbow, feeling it was night. Next I felt water under my feet. Then I was hit in the face with what seemed a bucketful. Then I began to hear the little falls right in front of me. I had run into a little falls of water. I nearly drowned in it, floundering about in the pool below, feeling for the ground and heaving my rifle in that direction out of the wet. I felt pleased to hear it land solid and not too hard. I then floundered again, merely feeling and knowing it was water.

I was careful drinking a little at a time. But then I got off my shirt, and held on to the bank of the little pool, lying in the water. I knew it would at present do the most good, soaking it up from the outside, instead of horse-wallering with my mouth as I had seen animals do and dying. My eyes got a little better then and there was shine above, either moon or stars, I could not tell which. So I saw a little rock shelf toward the downslope and went down there and laid down.

-6-

NEW ACQUAINTANCES
FOR LOHMAN

The first thing I knew the next day was the old man yelling. Then I saw him on a horse and a girl riding a mule with him and behind them a pack pony. They both started yelling. What I had taken for a rock shelf was part of a horse trail and I was laid right across it.

The old man yelled again, and then the girl threw something at me when I rose half up. I ducked, thinking it was a stone, but it was just a piñon nut. Now I saw the hill trail.

The old man stopped yelling when I closed my eyes and flopped back, not being able to speak yet but thinking, "Well, ride over me, you old fool."

I heard him say to the girl: "He's hurt."

I could hear them get off their mounts. Then I opened one eye enough to see the old man over me and the girl dimly. The mule and the old man's horse stood, but the horse they were leading, the pack horse, reared, and she quietened him.

"What's the matter, Sonny?" This the old man said.

I tried to get on my feet, and then say something, when he said: "Na, na, na—just rest easy." He pushed me down.

After that it was vague and mixed. They gave me some water, then whiskey, then more water, then more whiskey. Then poured water on me gentle, then did something for my crease wound, then a blanket folded under my head, then one under me.

Someone must have come along the trail later, because I could hear the old man giving them fits about going around me. He made them circle me and then get back on the hard road, and it sounded like quite a few horses, but I never knew.

But I judged that he felt it was lucky for them to come along. He got more whiskey for me from these strangers, though I could hardly get it down, and gave up a lot. I have never cared for taste nor effect of whiskey, even when sick.

I slept then awhile and when I woke the dark was coming down. I talked a little then and explained to them about my crease wound. They moved me near the fire they had made and then the old man came and squatted down.

"Yes, you've got a crease wound, but in the back of your thigh you were hit twice, and probably didn't realize it so there is a bullet hole and a ball under the crease. It's a wonder how you got this far from what you said."

I told him to get the ball.

He went to the pack and got out one of these old muzzle loaders. He let me heft it and look at it. It had the champion long barrel. The stock was pretty and polished. The stock-shank where your hand goes was carved like the neck of a goose head and feathers.

"Yep," the old man said, "like they call it, a goose gun. Curio. Taking it to a man I know."

He unscrewed the metal part of the ramrod and laid her in the fire, and he and the girl began to go after the bullet. Between groans, I said: "How you trying to go for it?"

The old man said he was kneading for it. He explained it was near the surface and they were trying to squeeze it like a boil to make it back out.

"Cut it," I said, "depending on the ball, it may have spread-eagled."

"Yes," said the old man, "we'll have to cut it a little."

After all that pinching I hardly felt the cut, but when he used the hot ramrod in the long hole I must have screamed so they could hear me at Socorro. I could smell my own meat frying. Being weak, I possibly fainted and did not wake up till next morning.

My crease wound then felt like it was filled with acid, but being stronger I was able to stand it then without much fuss. They had corn with them besides the horse feed and the girl was making thick corn cakes in the skillet, then cutting from a bacon slab, cooking it in with the corn. I could see now she was a good-looking girl about 19 or 20.

The old man had something yellow in his hand. Later he gave me pieces of it. It was an orange, second I had ever seen but never eaten.

"Californio," said the old man, and repeated it several times and then begun singing some kind of song in Spanish.

One thing I noticed the girl wore was a silver letter H made kind of crude like Mex work always seems, and I thought it stood for her name at first. She later did not wear this pin and still later on did wear it and I found out after she was having some trouble with the way the clasp worked on the pin back and so I fixed it for her. It was very plain on her dress, this pin.

I worked into that food all right. I was feeling good and sat up and talked to them both. When I tried it, I could move, but my thigh was still stiff with some swelling.

When I got to my feet, this was at the point the old man said to the girl: "We'll wait here for the people from the Boyds."

My rifle was laying over my half saddlebag and I reached for it.

Never saw anyone hook a gun so fast as the old man. He shirt-carried a four. I had seen mostly fives. There I was half leaning toward my rifle, and the old man had thrown down on me.

The girl threw her head back and laughed. Then she gave me a hateful look.

I smiled at the old man and said: "Small muzzle."

"Yep, it is," said the old man. "Sit down, Bub. I just took lead out of you, I don't want to pour any in."

There was a long quiet after this, the old man appearing to be thinking. Then he said aloud, "Some misunderstanding here," as if to himself. The girl said nothing.

Right then I had my first real chance to study them good.

He looked about 60 and I hoped I would be as good at that age. Found later he was 71. He was wiry. He had small, blue eyes like Mr. Restow's, and wore his clothes loose. He wore fringed pants with the hind part out like an Indian or like chaps. He wore wonderful moccasins of the plains type with hard soles to protect against the cactus.

They had hill patterns around the base of the uppers and Trails of Life painted on their instep. Some high-type squaw may have mixed the decorations a little but she surely knew how to make moccasins. His shirt was heavy, Spanish cut with neck strings.

The girl she wore a blue dress, of the prettiest dark blue I ever saw, hung a little short to show her legs which was unusual and which I could see was bare above the knee, and high Indian leggins that covered her well and made her decent. She might have been older than 20, even 22. Her hair was black and back tight. Her skin on her face and neck seemed soft and bright. Her eyes were black. That girl was in good health. She was part Spanish sure, but maybe a little more mestizo. When she smiled her teeth looked better even than false ones.

But she had no use for me. When the old man and I started talking again, she listened. Then she turned up her nose and laughed and said, "Kill him and be done with it, kill him," and moseyed up the rise, and begun to tease her horse with a mite of sugar. Finally she got on him and rode him out of sight.

I found that the mule she had rode was just for that day to ease the back of her horse after they had heavy-padded their more or less light pack on him. Their mule was really used for pack. When she had gone, the old man said maybe he could make her let me have her horse, or he would ride the mule, so we could all get along.

I said: "She'll give me nothing. She would do nothing for me."

7

LOHMAN DOES SOME SHOOTING

The old man laughed and said: "You kids are all alike. Can't wait for nothing. Everything has to be settled quick. Hell, Bub, I got to find out about you. These things take time."

I said nothing, not wishing to crowd him.

He said: "She's just a little crazy. All women are. My folks I married into are Spanish. Nearly all women at my ranchero. Hell of a situation. Like a harem. Took on a passel of women. I'm taking her up to St. Loo at a school the sisters have. If we leave her down here they are feared at home she might marry the first three-toed bush ape who comes along."

I thanked him for explaining.

He looked at me and squinted and said: "You are a kind of formal kid, ain't you? Well, we have some kind of family pride, having some connections with the Maxwells. Know the Maxwells?"

I said not.

He said: "They used to own hell of a lot of land around here. Much less now. Still it's considerable. Old Man Maxwell is mucha galoot."

He shoved his gun into his shirt. "Now just let your tale come out in chunks."

I told him my name. He said, "Oh, the Lohmans. Wasn't your father sheriff at Toscoso awhile back?"

I said yes that also two of my brothers, Nevin and Pete, had been peace officers.

"And where are they now?"

"They were both shot dead at age 21."

"You don't say." He looked at me hard. "Now let's see. Something comes back to me. Nevin Lohman. Why, he worked for Hunter Boyd once. Why, hell yes, I recall Nevin. Well, son of a gun!"

He was quiet a long time, thinking.

"How about you and the Boyds now? The way you growled around in your sleep."

I said the Boyds were looking for me.

"So I gather."

I told him they were people with easy-hurt pride.

"Oh I know the Boyds," he said. "They all walk with a short-dog strut."

I told him I had killed Shorty.

"Self-defense?"

"Yes."

"With a rifle-gun?"

I thought awhile and he waited politely. Then I said, "I'll tell you the real way it was. I was supposed to have shot Shorty Boyd, but did not. It was another way."

"Want to tell me?"

I told him I would. I told him I was left alone by my father with some people in central Texas he knew. Then I got my horse and rode up to see Mr. Restow about getting a job, on written advice of my father. I rode till late dark the second night getting up toward Twist and near the Restow ranch, and they was a schoolhouse on the road. I stopped to the schoolhouse and they was a dance going on, a scarcity of men and they asked me to stay.

I said I stood there because I did not know how to dance. Then this girl came along and asked. I refused. Then she asked me for a glass of water. When I got one for her here came the Boyds—Tom, Otis, Shorty and some cousins all drunk.

Shorty dared me outside and shot at me and this was the first I knew I had gotten water for his girl. But then his kin saw I was unarmed, and held him back. But they were mean-drunk and handed me a gun and Shorty who was never a shot and worse now with liquor shot at me again and I found my gun was empty.

I said that then I ran in the schoolhouse and Shorty followed me there. There was a candle stuck on a table there. It was stuck in a States War bayonet, and the bayonet point sunk in the tabletop. I grabbed the bayonet, as Shorty fired again and rushed me, and just about stabbed himself in the ruckus. Everybody gave out that I shot Shorty. He died the next day.

After I had stated this, which was true, the old man said nothing for a long time, just sat pulling out grass stems. He said: "Oh, it had to be bullets, being a gentleman's war." He laughed. "They are a mean crowd." He would look at me, then away. "If the Boyds come here I doubt I will give you to them. I doubt that."

I thanked him.

I told him then that Harley, the brother that had strayed off, we had not heard from in years. How Pete and Nevin had been shot. How I was riding to Socorro to help my father but now had no horse. I told him how Nevin was shot down near the Pecos, as far as we knew the facts. Then I recounted to him how after a long time my father sent me down there to get him dug up, bring him back and bury him on his own ground. And how Nevin's hair had growed in the box, so he looked like a man with a porkopine for a head.

He said: "How old were you when your father sent you on this joyful mission?"

I said 13. I then told him how my mother had died after the Comanches hit. How they had killed my baby sister Julia with an arrow. I explained that I felt since my father and I were all that was left we should be together.

"Yes," he said, looking at me. "Yes, I would be inclined to agree."

He leaned forward and said: "Would the name be originally Tate?"

I said yes, Tot for Tate. Then told him how I had hokused the Boyds and spooked their herd. He said "Well, well." Then he got up, handed me my gun and said, "Let me see how you work her."

Well, I did it to please him, not wanting to shoot for show. I shot some chips off trees and such, laying them in close and calling the shots. Then nudging stones near the falls little by little till they fell in the water. I hip shot the rifle for him.

He kept saying "Well, well." Finally he put out his hand, took mine, and said, "Lohman, I am Amos Bradley. I have seen some shooting in my time—and I would call this fair, fair, jest fair." Then he laughed fit to kill. "You brag too much, Bub." Then again he laughed hard. "At last I have met up with a man who can hunt cockroaches with a rifle—ever try fleas?"

Well, that is an old high plains joke, and I laughed at it to please Mr. Bradley who had been so kind to me.

"How about you and me hunting some day?" he said.

I said I would as a favor, as I did not hunt much. I told him my father had been the finest standing shot with a rifle I had ever seen, and had trained all of us and that Nevin had been pretty good with a pistol.

"Hunt with me as a favor?" He looked at me careful. "You Quaker stock?"

I said my mother had been a Quaker. He seemed interested. So I told him how she had come to the west with my father, with a hank of cotton thread, one of linen and one of silk, a carven cradle, a silk dress and two poetry books, one by the writer Milton.

"Diluted some, I see," he said.

I said my father had been raised for a minister-like and sung hymns a lot. He looked at me very sharp and said, "Mother sing them?"

I said no, but she liked to listen to them.

Mr. Bradley said as we began to move back that he had once taught school back east. He hummed to himself. Then he said: "I know a bit more about your father than you think, but was holding back to see how you would talk. I think he is working for an outfit that is not too-good managed and owned by an Englishman. It is called the T Cross T. It is a registered brand but this man who owns her is sort of a too-nice fellow and I am told has some pretty shady galoots on his string. They say they are former cow-lifters. I would not know. Your father ought to get out of there and from what I hear I would advise moving him further south for his health as he has this wasting sickness. Why he wants to cook for a crowd of no-good cowpokers who have badmen among them is more than I can understand."

I said then I understood my father had done some favors for the owner and the owner was giving him plenty of light work and even leaving him off the cooking when necessary. I said to Mr. Bradley that this was what I had been told by the man at the Silver Spur.

We started back, becoming a little worried then about the girl, and I said I would climb a rise and scan around for her. While I was doing this, Mr. Bradley poked up the fire a little and folded up some blankets and started to nose-bag the mule, and here came Hunter Boyd up among the trees.

I recognized Old Man Boyd because I had seen him once before. He was on a big roan, leading another horse up from the canyon and had come on us sudden-like. Scared, I begun to edge down from the trees toward my gun.

I heard him tell Amos that two of his hands would meet them the next day to lead them up through the poor country. Amos kept motioning me down. I came down finally, edging over near my rifle.

Old Man Boyd backed his horse a little and looked at me through slitted eyes. He might have been heavy when young, but now was thinning out with age. Hair was pure white. He had the deepest creases I ever saw from nose to mouth-corner. His right arm was helpless from an elbow gunshot wound that had been froze in a blizzard and proud-fleshed after. He held the reins in the crook of that elbow, with the hand tarnally straight up like a steel claw.

He looked me over from head to foot, then turned away. Everything was quiet. His Colt was straight up beside the horn in a wide-flap holster. First I had ever seen a gun on a saddle peak. I watched his left hand.

Then I looked at Amos, and it was surprising how he had changed. He had walked over, leaned down and put his gun in his shirt. When he rose up, his eyes had changed. They were like needle points, and his frame looked like a cocked gun. He said: "This is my guest."

Old Man Boyd licked his chops. I kept watch of him. I saw how thin his thigh was under the shiny-wore leather pants. The white fleece under the saddle skirt matched his hair. The horn was low, with silver on top big as a tin dish.

He said: "Ease yourself, Amos."

There was a long quiet. Then he said: "Seems like a cap of rain due."

"Sure does," said Amos. "We could use her."

There was another quiet spell. Long.

"Saw a girl on a horse when I came up here. Might that be your child you spoke of?"

"True," said Amos, "and whiles we're on that, just to keep everybody bellied up to the bar for treats, this here is Tot Lohman. He had a hard time over by the dry. But now I believe is fit to travel on. He seems a gentle boy, not one to brag-shoot nor flounce about killing people."

"Good for him. I knew he was here. My men told me, which is why I came over. He is the Tot Lohman that killed my son Shorty, and stampeded my hill strays when Otis and Tom were foolishing around with them over near the state line. His father was known somewhat to me. So was his brother, Nevin, who was a good boy."

Then I said the only words I used in the whole talk.

"Nevin was shot dead."

For a long time Old Man Boyd said nothing, just keeping his eyes off me and far away. You could have heard a cricket rustle with the wind down in the jacks. All of a sudden Old Man Boyd threw the rope of the led-horse to Amos.

"That is Tot Lohman's horse, so give it to him. Let him get a fair start. My sons should of shot him, and I could now— maybe. But it is not going to be said of my family that they got knocked around by a squirt who is gifted with a rifle, then shot his horse fifty, seventy-five miles from water. The Boyds are not horse-killers."

"Well, thank you kindly," said Amos, "this'll get him to Socorro."

"Yes," said Old Man Boyd. "I understand he is headed there, as his father is in some difficulty, so Henry DeChute tells me. Well, since he can't burrow down there like a mole or snake, he'd better sleep on his stomach and ride on the far side of his horse, because my sons will trail him from here to hell and back. He'll never cross the river. I doubt if he fetches Las Vegas."

He turned his horse then and we saw him go down under the trees out of sight.

8

CAMP HAS SOME MORE VISITORS

After Old Man Boyd left we began to think about the girl. Pretty soon here she came riding down the dry, like as she had found a steep switch-off from the hill road further back.

First thing she said was: "Where'd you get the horse?" Amos explained to her. "It's a good thing," she said. "I'd have never given him mine to go on. He'd have had to take the mule. He'd look right on a mule."

Amos said: "It's about time you dropped that smart talk. Rustle around now and heave some grits together. And no back talk. We get an early start in the morning. Boyd's men will take us further up the road. If I recall rightly it begins to look like a road on up from here."

I was feeling the horse, whose rope I now held. He had a wild black eye and showed a good deal of red around the rim. But I gentled him down and would work some more on that. He was a fine horse, the finest I had ever seen, a little small and light but well-boned but too light for general cattle work.

I gave him a drink at the falls. I got a rag and wiped him down. He stood well. Then I gave him a mite of sugar I begged from Amos, who gave it to me as if he was sore without looking at me. He was deep-thinking about something. Amos also gave me some of his writing stuff, when I told him I sorely missed the cut-off saddlebag. He gave me a pencil also as mine was lost. He had rode back the first day to see if he could pick up some of my lost stuff and had found a little.

All our thoughts now were on moving the next day.

The girl, whose name I now knew, was frying bacon in the spider, and I said to her: "Nita, if you will let that off the fire a little, I'll rake in the coals and make it easier for you." She was cooking on a too-high fire and getting singed and didn't know it.

She jumped like a shot when I used her name, and said something under her breath. Amos had had me worried, thinking he might be angry at me about something, but he looked up suddenly at this and gave the girl a look and said: "Now that is a nice friendly way to get along, first-naming each other, and see that you kids keep it up. His name is Tot, so begin acting as if you wouldn't bite each other."

Right then I began to realize that I had been standoffish also, never dreaming that I had. But the girl needed a lot more gentling, because she slammed the spider around, slammed the coffee-pot lid, and sort of threw herself in the middle with her hips, but she did back off from the fire.

I cleaned it up then, as she was a straggle-fire maker, and I brushed the edges and raked up the coals and sorted out stuff. Then I got a fork-stick that was good and green and laid it on stones. She put the coffee pot then on the little end of the fork, and laid the spider on the big end. She then began really to cook.

I thought next Amos had gone crazy because he hopped down from the rise where he'd been scanning, got the axe and began to chop dirt as fast as he could, talking to himself, swearing, and yelling to me to get something to dig with.

The girl slicked the food off the blaze and we both began to help Amos throw dirt onto the fire, fast as we could, because now I knew and so did the girl what Amos was driving at.

We got the smoke killed off quick, but the fire took more time. But we deadened her, except for ash, and Amos was already moving up the slope.

I looked at Nita. She was ransacking the saddle gear for shell-boxes. I got all the shell I thought I'd need from the pile Amos had left after the shooting.

Then I started up after Amos. The girl hung back, but she had found an extra Colt for Amos. We were situated on a slope that tended to the north, in the opposite direction from where Old Man Boyd had gone. But beyond the rubble and talus stuff down toward the dry, the foot of the hill opened out and around to a low place with a lot of rock in it. This level ran away from us for nearly a mile, or maybe nearer a mile and a half, and beyond that was steep slopes and steeper bluffs running straight up to the rimrock.

We snaked around among the biggest rocks. Then I saw the most remarkable sight you can believe. They were on the high bluffs. The sun to the west was under a cloud, heavy-like, so their shapes were shadowy and they seemed part of the mountain. There must have been at least two hundred of them on ponies and for a while the only way you could tell them from stone statues was the way the wind sometimes lifted the longer tails of the pintos. They saw us. It was easy to see us but they never moved.

Then the wind began to blow from up there, and the sun came out a little and you could see the shine on their carbines, and the shine on some of the shell and bead work of the chiefs and even the shine of skin on their faces and thighs, and of the silver stuff they wore. The wind began to bring their smell to us, like a fox or a bear smell, specially a bear when he has just swum a creek.

I came out with the word, "Comanches," as they were the Indians I had chiefly known.

Amos said: "No, they're not. Utes."

The girl behind us with the extra Colt and the shell began to cry, and Amos snapped: "Stop that." She dried up then. I began to feel sorry for her.

She must have felt I was softer than Amos because she started wiggling toward me between rocks, and then she curled up about a foot from me, and I reached back my hand and waved it to her. "Don't worry," I said. "Your father and I will take care of this. So don't fret."

It was the way I recall my brother Nevin talking to my mother the day the Comanches hit our place.

Amos said after a little, as the seconds dragged out, "Pshaw, I don't think they're going to do anything but look at us. But they're looking for somebody. We're small meat compared to what they're after. I wonder what son of a bitch supplied the fire-water for *this* sortie."

After a while of waiting, Amos said: "I thought so. All right, we'll handle them. You better forget you're a Quaker, Bub, because we've got to stop a few."

Now I saw what his eyes had been quicker to see than mine. There was a long shale slope down to the left of us and down that what looked like four came on pintos, the horses jiggling their hind ends up and down as they half-scrambled, half-fell down the slope.

Amos grumbled. "Maybe the damn fools'll kill their-selves on that deal."

But they didn't. All got down all right. Then they powwowed. "Oh must talk it over now," said Amos, "must talk it over—make big talk—ketchum white man—scalpum plenty—come on, let's get it over."

Amos had a pair of glasses. He had bit off a little chew, that I'd never seen him use before and he was chewing fast, and we passed the glasses back and forth.

He said: "Well, one thing we can be thankful for. Glad they've taken up new ways. Those aren't young braves. In the old days the braves would make the rush which I calculate is jest for the hell of it. But those I see are plain bums." Then he spit: "Those of the noble redskins who can be spared."

The Indians were still talking.

"Let's see what we have here," said Amos. "They'll not circle, not enough of them. We have two Colts and one rifle. Nita can't shoot. They'll come in a straight rush, head on, just to show the boys on the hills how brave they are. They've done something shameful in the tribe and this is how they will try to live it down. I'll bet the old chief up there has a grin on his face . . ." Mr. Bradley was talking and joking because he was nervous.

So then on they came. Amos yelled to me to take the two on the right and he'd watch the two left. But a surprising thing happened. They could shoot. They began to fire at us straight off, and they were a lot better with those bead-traded carbines than I'd of expected. Stones began to fly around among us, and the top of the rock Nita and I lay behind began to act as if it was alive.

"Come on," Amos yelled, and began to fire his Colt in all directions, it seemed to me. The girl handed him the other, and reloaded the first fast.

I waited and got my sights down at about 45 yards and aimed low and leftwards and the one in front when I shot went sailing right over the pony's head, because the pony made a quick stop. Sighting down on the other I first hit his horse by mistake and then with a very lucky angling shot I knocked the front of his face in. It was terrible to see. That Indian's features seemed to fly forty ways.

But the other dehorsed one I was going to put another shot in. But he rolled on the ground and I put down my gun because I saw he had a very bad shoulder wound. Amos was yelling and still firing off the second load of the first gun.

But the other two didn't require it. Their little paint horses put down their stiff front legs and began sliding. The air that had been loud for a while turned quiet.

One of the braves not hit came up. Then the other. Then they dismounted, put the dead one across his pony that they had to catch first, helped the wounded one up on his saddle, waited for him to fall off. He fell off. So then they picked him up and started going back. They were so near we could see their face paint.

Amos scratched the hairs on his chin, "Hell," he said, "I guess it's all over. Kinda disappointed."

I said I was not disappointed at all, and he smiled at me.

"Should think not. The help I gave you. All I did was yell and bang off."

I said mine were easy shots. Amos said he knew that. But he said: "I was shooting like a beer-drunk cowhand, supported by the genuine confidence you inspire."

It took me a little time to separate this. Every once in a time he would talk like a book. I said it would have been an easy shot for him, too, if he'd had a rifle.

"Yes," Amos said, "I expect it would. But don't try telling me any normal man can shoot a rifle-gun like you. Don't go polite on me."

We were still nervous and the girl had lagged behind. She was back of us near the big stone. Or that seemed the way it happened. She was picking up spent shell to be sure none of them were good ones. This Amos probably had taught her.

A fifth Ute, one we had not seen, was on a horse like the rest, only he must have paced him up slow on the shade side of the big rock, for all of a sudden he was above her on his pinto, trying to grab her up, and she was screaming and hitting at him. He had a rifle but he wasn't intending to use it evidently. Because he kept hacking at her with a hand-axe, the crude kind they carry, and missing her. He was not yelling nor speaking but just silently wanting to get her.

I dove for the horse's hind legs in fear. I was trying to throw both pinto and rider, and I remember how, as I grabbed the hocks low, I saw the hoofs were muffle-shod. It was bark or something that looked like crude cloth.

It was not such a bad move. I'd done the same before, horsing around with kids back home. You sort of hamstring a pony in fun, making him near sit and throw the rider off.

But Amos dove high for the rider and was around his waist. That old man could fight and be mean. I saw him working from below while I hung on to the pony's back legs. He was trying to reach the brave's knife. Even from under I could smell the Indian smell strong.

Amos hogged him high, I hogged him low, the horse started to sit down, the brave slid back. I then grabbed him around the neck from behind. Amos got back some and on balance and gave him another rush. We held him down while Amos beat in his head with a rock.

I looked and saw Amos breathing hard, tears coming out of his eyes. He staggered around groaning, pulling at his chest. The girl was halfway between a sweat and the screaming fantods, but she ran like a deer back up the rise and brought down a bottle of whiskey for Mr. Bradley. He quieted a little after the whiskey, but complained of heart pains. Then he took another swig and felt better. The Indians on the bluff started to move along. It seemed about over.

We got back to our place and saw the whole crowd on the rim move out of sight. We were worried for a while, then ate, and Amos said: "Well, I made you kill today, Bub, and it probably is just as well you did, aside from the idea killing a man is not like killing an Indian."

I said I thought Indians were men. He grunted and said: "Maybe so—looks also as if you might have to fight your way down there through the Boyds."

Said I did not want to kill any Boyds.

"You may not, but it appears they want to kill you, which makes it complicated."

We rebuilt the fire finally. Amos said he thought the Utes were trying to dodge a platoon of the 9th Cavalry sent to shoo them in, but were picking up a horse where they could. They had been considering other more important things than us, but it was just as well all told they did not spot our horses. They might have taken all. Not the mule. Indians do not seem to care for mules. I never saw a mule and an Indian together.

To help his heart, Amos had drunk considerable, but now did not stop. He grew very talkative. He kept sucking at that bottle. I refused a drink but Nita took a sip. It was then I noted her right hand behind her, and when I spoke of it she started yelling and crying. Amos snatched at her hand. She had balled up a strip of cloth inside her fist to soak up the blood. Right through the leftwards side of her hand there was a bullet hole. It was the only blood the Utes drew on us.

She was afraid of being burned with the ramrod. But she let us wash and dress the hole, which was as clean a wound as I ever saw. She whimpered a little when Amos soaked a cloth in something he had in a bottle and ran it through her hand.

But then he motioned toward the goose gun. We had to run that little squaw all over the mountain, dodging behind trees. She kept up her yelling. At last Amos caught her.

She kept hitting him and crying. It touched me a good deal. Amos pointed out to me that the hole was a clean one, fresh made, not like mine. The heat of the slug going through had probably cleaned it up enough. We did finally get a bandage on it.

Amos told me how to do it, so I axed off a little branch of oak or pine, I forget which, and shaped her down to a kind of square block and strapped it down but not too tight. But Amos warned her if there was a smell or least sign in the morning, he would have to stick her with the ramrod.

She was gentled down then. I cooked the supper.

After supper Amos then told Nita he wanted to show me something, so we jigged up the fire and left her there, walking to a big rise but where we could see her. We kept a close watch of her. We had our guns with us, and left her with the Colt. We had seen no signs of Utes but were taking no chances.

"Now there—look over there," Amos said.

I looked and saw a little grab of lights on the plain.

"Now that is Clayton. She's on high ground so you can see her quite a while. That is your bearing point for a starter. Keep that on the left of your tail as long as you can. Maybe even at night you can get up a rise and see her quite a ways down. I would not know. But anyway that will be for a starter." He pointed south and west. "Now if you go too far west, the first thing you may notice is a kind of runty hill that looks like a covered wagon. You can't miss that if you ride fairly near. For me, if I was you, I would keep to the center of things. The Boyds might figger you would parallel the Santa Fe trail south, but they don't like riding rough ground any better than you do. You have got a bigger reason than they to move slower through struck-up country. Down mostly directly south of us is some caves where gas comes from the ground. You may probably see them.

"The way I figger it you should out to shoot straight south for Santa Rosa. Minute you get there, get to my casa and hand the stuff I've written to the womenfolks. Now the towns you will want to avoid—like Springer and Maxwell—they are far to the west from where I am aiming to send you. Now if I was you I would shack up a whiles with this sheepherder I know. I wrote his name down back there on that stuff I fixed for you. His name is Bawbeen. Remember that. Bawbeen. He'll do anything for me."

I asked him if the man's name was Irish, as it sounded so.

"No," said Amos, "it is French. Maybe I don't give it the proper sound but it's near enough. Everybody calls him that, and he's known all through the country there, even up here. He'll give you the right steer and will not let down on you."

I said I understood.

"Now," he said further, "just before you fetch Santa Rosa, which is nearly all Mex, you'll find a little place called Anton Chico. If you get there there is one saloon and a bartender I know. I gave you a note for him. He can't read but will get someone to read it for him. The real name of the place is Sangre de Cristo, which means Blood of Christ. But that is too much of a mouthful for irreligious, ignorant people like us so we call it Anton Chico. The reason I advise against Fort Union is that the Boyds will surely scout up the place, and no telling what they might say. The military might get to pondering about you. However, that's for you to decide. Just one thing, if you hit the fort or the hill that looks like a prairie schooner, you will be too near the trail. Better ease off to the eastward and middle part. At Santa Rosa they will tell you whether to take the north or south pass to Socorro."

I told him I understood and he made me a map.

He said: "The Boyds have a lot of people depending on them for a living, and that gives them plenty of room to work. Then they have a lot of small-fry relations, ranging from poor to well-to-do. If it's a Big Hunt, you'll find out soon by the amount of money they throw out, for they got plenty of that same stuff. But I just figure you are a boy who is not to be fooled with much with shooting-weapons. I figger that word has kind of gotten around. I know I would not want to fool much with you. Now this Bawbeen, he is on the good side of the cattlemen because he traps wolves for them, but he hates cattlemen just the same because he is a sheepman. Also in killing wolves, recollect he is at the same time protecting his sheep. I know he hates the Boyds from something away back. I know Old Man Maxwell likes him."

We walked back to the fire and the girl.

Amos had been writing some stuff before supper, but now he started writing again with a pencil so old and small you could hardly see it in his hand. He wrote notes for me to take, and gave me paper and another dinky pencil when I begged them off him. From back when my father wanted me to make a sale-list of stuff from our farm when it was sold, harness, tools and all, I had tried to keep a record of myself without more than half regularity, but now caught up some with what I had been through. Amos had good, ruled paper for me to write on, but the pencil wore down fast. When I looked up from what I was trying to put down, Amos was taking off his moccasins and jacket, and next rolled up in a horse blanket and started snoring to wake the dead.

In my sleep that night there was a weight on my chest. I woke up fast, and the girl Nita was bending over me and I wondered did I dream that she kissed me, but then she proved it by doing it again.

When I started to say something she let me have her block-splinted hand right across the mouth hard. Then she kissed me again and kept saying, "Keep still—keep quiet." She talked through her teeth as if she was angry.

I was never so surprised. I moved enough to look at Amos. He was complete out with the whiskey.

Now I knew she was crazy. She went back under the tent lining she was using that night. I lay listening to the wind in the jacks. I could again see her hot, beautiful eyes and feel her wet mouth.

I dozed off. But I was not to sleep much that night. Amos jerked my arm. I thought it was morning. I heard him say: "I want to talk to you." So then I got awake and rose up gradually.

Walked to the fire he had jigged up. Refused a drink from the bottle. He took a swig and said: "Sit down, I want to talk to you. I am concerned."

Then he said nothing. I sat there rubbing my eyes and listening to the wind. Finally he said: "Listen, you will never make Socorro. Bub, I cotton to you. Come on up northways with the girl and me."

I shook my head.

"You can easy take the stage line. And with her in St. Loo, you can get something for a whiles to occupy you. You will never make Socorro and are worth saving. You know somewhat but you are a green kid."

He took a swig: "This here is uncivilized country. Over there in your native Texas they don't kill a man except about once a month or so, but over here they kill all the while. There is cattle rustling, stealing money, claim jumping, whoring around and a right deal of degeneracy. Over there they have the old West Texas crowd. Then they have some native people too who are sad because they missed the education in crime the others got in West Texas. But they tried hard and just developed their own brand of orneriness. And they are doing well, I hear. Doing well. They tell me they have some of the Dillons over there, and one of the Jameses. But just for show, you understand. They have a good deal of pride in their meanness and want to advertise it. They don't entirely need fancy reputations to help them. There are people I know of there that I actually do not want to meet— anywhere. And you don't know how mean I can get when sore.

Rather than meet these people I would prefer Injuns. And also, the Boyds would not stop at hiring a whole town to turn out and kill you, if you keep pushing of them. Stop pushing. Just ease yourself and come up north with me."

I said nothing but showed him I was interested.

"Now to show you the Boyds. When you were still standing away from Hunter and me today, know what he told me? When Tom Boyd came home a few days back from the trouble you made him, Old Man Boyd larruped him with an alder cane. Whopped him, larruped him. Growed man, twenty-two, twenty-three years old. He said to me 'I busted two canes on him, Amos, and grabbed for the third.' Now I show you this to show you the Boyds. You think you are tough. To them you are baby-soft."

I told Amos how I had figured the Boyds. That they were always out to take something from somebody. I told him how I had figured the Boyds back by the dry.

"Yes," he said, "they are gettin'-people."

I told Amos I had to help my father.

"You can't help him if you die, Bub."

I agreed to this.

"How much do you value your life?"

I said I would have to think that over.

"Think it over?" He spit, took a swig and said: "Now I know you're crazy."

I asked Amos if he thought the dead are happy.

He gave me a sour look and said he would have to think that one over.

Finally he said: "Well, Bub, I warned you."

Then I told him what I had decided: "No more of this

foolishing around with scare-shots and cattle. I will shoot first from now on and will aim for one of two places, the head or the heart."

Amos looked at me a long time. "Well," he finally said, "if you aim at either one, you kill a man as a rule, and you don't have to prove to me that you can hit where you aim. I hope you get a bag-ful of Boyds. But in the end they'll get you. Yep."

We rolled up then and went to sleep.

Amos was sore and touchy when we called him and cussed a lit-tle but he at length got up. He kept groaning and rubbing his face with his hands. Then as it got lighter, the gray sliding down south and west among the canyons, he had a drink he called doghair which was no different from the others. Sat looking at the fire and finally went to the falls to fill the cans and bags.

He stayed a long while there, and she came down to me and said she now knew both my names and liked Tot better than Bub. She wanted to give me the pin like an H. And here she had melted it on a split stick in the fire and torn off the one bar of the H, as cattle-men do to change a brand, and it was now a T. I just stared at her. She then calmly lifted up her blue skirt showing her beautiful white thigh well above her knee-high leggins and then said that crazy girl, "I will brand myself T and I will be Tot Lohman's girl forever."

I grabbed her and held her, feeling sick, but also having another feeling. She was hurt when I grabbed her hard, and squealed a little—Amos looked back from the falls in time to see her lean in to me right under my chin and then reach up and kiss me long and good. I was afraid but Amos just smiled and went back to can filling.

I told her she was crazy but I took the pin and put it under my shirt—on the left side as she wanted, she reaching in and closing the clasp of the pin herself, then patting my bare chest under the pocket there. But when she moved I ducked away so she could not kiss me again, feeling sure Amos might forgive us once, but might after then be scandalized. Amos had been very kind to me, and I wanted to show him plenty of respect, and the thought came to me, What would my people think of all this?

When we were ready to start and part, I was sad, but Amos kept drawing it out. Nita sat her pony awhile looking at him and me. I did not want to mount until he was ready to go with politeness and he kept sitting there at the fire with a few more drinks going down now and again.

"Amos," she kept saying. "Amos."

Shortly he put the bottle away, roused up and together we killed the fire, but while we did he said: "The little grain and stuff you borrowed from us, and the pair of saddlebags to go with your cut one, you can pay back someday."

I said yes sir.

"Sorry you will have to ride blanket and strap, but I have no saddle to spare."

I told him that was all right.

He was dousing the last of the fire.

"Anybody ever tell you what color your eyes are?"

Well, now that is a strange thing for one man to say to another but I knew how much he had drunk, though in all movements he was perfectly steady and sure.

I said I thought they tended to be blue.

"Bet Nita knows."

She turned red like fire there in the saddle.

Amos laughed at her and then me. "Yes, they are blue but there is a kind of smoky color in them. This morning I am just thin-minded enough to see it good."

I looked at the sun and said the light was getting better.

"Ever been mad in your life, Tot?"

I said sure.

"But ever real good and mad? I ask this because I don't think you have and are a cool galoot for one of your age."

Told him I did not really know.

"Well, I know," he said. "I know. You have possibly never been really good and mad, but when that day comes I do not want to be around. No sir, I do not want to be around whether you have anything to shoot with or not at that time. I will fix it to be in other parts of the country. But there is no reason why I should not try to imagine what your eyes will look like at that moment, no sir."

He took a long swig of liquor and then began to look at the bottle and then to mumble to himself.

He got on his horse. I got on mine, he said goodbye to me still with the mumbling voice but once he turned and smiled and waved his hand. Nita swung in behind then. The pack mule started after her. She turned and called good luck.

I felt bad when I turned my little horse down the steep, with a blanket and surcingle under me, and with two borrowed saddlebags from Amos and my own. I had that pin, which I could feel cold against my chest. I watched them moving out. I never felt so bad.

9

LETTER FROM AMOS BRADLEY TO HENRY RESTOW

Dear Henry Restow: Though it has been a long, long time since we met, I believe you will recall me, as I do you. I am giving this letter to one of the Boyd riders tomorrow, on the chance that he is drifting over to the state line and might drop it to one of your boys. This Lohman Kid with whom I have spent several days—why did you let him get away from your ranchero to descend on me? I have had the responsibility of looking after him and my daughter for a few days, and I sat up most of the night trying to argue with the crazy Kid that he should not ride south to certain death. But it was no use. He has one idea on his mind which is to get to his father, who I understand is mixed up in his life, his health and his thinking, as he is cooking for this Britisher Gerard who is getting off the lawside without probably knowing it.

But I could not tell all these matters to the Kid, not being sure of some of them. You know how Dame Rumor has a way of getting things twisted. But I did make it perfectly plain to the Young Man that he has about as much chance of reaching Socorro as a rabbit has of killing a wolf.

The terrible thing about all this is that I have grown fond of this boy—never having had a son of my own—and he is worth saving. This boy is not a bad boy. Luck merely has been against him. He is underneath some crudities a manly boy. He is all right. He has been kind to me and my daughter, after meeting up with us, though that is not the way to put it. What happened was we pulled him back from the brink of the grave, finding him horseless and having had no food or water for days. The Boyds shot his horse and he walked I don't know how far across the dry. When we found him it was just in time. A couple more hours and I believe he would have cashed in.

It is much on my mind that I have not told him all that Boyd told me. They are determined to get the boy between here and his destination and as for his father, they probably figure on hitting the father through the boy or vice versa. You know the Boyds and how they think, except that they don't think. It seemed to me that if I made it too strong to the boy he would be more determined. But on the other side it was the consideration of warning him enough for his own safety. The Boyds have got it firm in their minds that the boy is a crazy killer. Or they merely pass this out to ease their consciences and set the country against him.

Just wanted you to know I did all I could.

Amos Bradley.

P.S. I am giving this sealed to possibly, as I said, a Boyd rider. Two weeks ago I would have been reluctant to do so. But now I feel differently. If they want to break the seal and read it I do not give a good god damn.

-10-

LOHMAN TURNS SOUTH

I looked back at the Bradleys. Could still see the pack mule and Amos on the horse, but not Juanita. Then I got sight of her riding ahead and her blue dress. They passed the ridge and went out of sight.

Turning Blacky around, I rode a mile south then through the morning haze. I looked back after I had come up a rise, but could not see the Bradleys, but saw something else. A man was ambling his horse around the hill corner.

I picked a pine screen and rode to a higher rise. The man had stopped his horse and was off tightening his cinches. He had a large powerful black stallion made heavier than Blacky. His saddle was Mex made heavy.

I knew him right off. His name was Hal Carmody, a big powerful, expert cow wrangler on the Marcus order. He had been assistant foreman for the Boyds, but now had become, I heard, a kind of bodyguard to Old Man Boyd, riding some places with him. When he got on again, he held himself in the saddle like a man who sees everything and means business.

Did not like having him on my trail. Wanted no truck with him. He was a crack shot and expert roper and knew the country, I could see.

I walked Blacky from the off side of the rise and kept slogging. Walked the back trail to make sure he was not dogging to throw my attention from the road ahead. There might be people ahead waiting, for this is an old trick.

Twice I took advantage of the hilly country, showing myself to him plain, seeing I was following a half-fresh trail of plenty of hoof marks. I would show myself, then ride left hard through a small canyon and watch him rush past. He was too anxious, and thought it would be easy.

Up ahead he would stop, realize his mistake and then double back, but by that time I had left the canyon same way I came in and had rode hard sometimes two miles to the rear all under cover. Then I would wide-circle him to get on his front.

Twice I did that. He was getting pretty sore.

Then he changed his plan. For a long time I did not see him, because now he was keeping himself hid. But I would find a half-hid place, stand easy and wait for the wind and hear his horse. He had made a mistake using the stud stallion. There were a few wild horses in the region and the stallion smelled them. The stallion whinnered a good deal, which helped me.

An hour after noon when the country got flatter for a while and tree-scarce, I saw him plain from seven miles off. Now he had another man with him. The new man I did not recognize. They exchanged horses and I saw Carmody mount again. I saw the other man lead the stallion back toward the hills and saw why.

The stallion was limping. He may have struck a gopher hole. But Carmody was a smart man and must have had two reasons for changing mounts, the limp and the noise of the rutty horse.

But now I knew two things. As Bradley said, they were getting the hunt organized big with relay horses. Also they had decided to ride me down, like wild horses are wore out.

I was glad to see the stallion limping. It showed me I was right in thinking Carmody was too anxious, too confident and pushing reckless and hard.

As night came down I struck a grab of trees, as I kept drifting east in my drive south, having seen the wagon-shaped hill Bradley told me about. I wanted to sheer off the Santa Fe trail somewhat at least. I found the natural cave where Bradley had told me gas was coming out of the ground.

Rode Blacky up close to a hole where there was no gas I could smell. I dismounted but he backed and snorted. Then I pushed but he blew hard through his nose. Then I grabbed his ears and held his head down till all he could see was ground. Then he carne on in gently.

He had only been afraid of bumping his head on the low mouth of the place. I tied him, hoping he would stay quiet.

Then I came out of the place, cut back and climbed a tree. I waited what must have been two hours for Carmody. At first I heard his horse way west. Then he doubled back. Then he circled in the dark, trying to pick up my marks. Then he circled nearer me. I was getting nervous.

He had a light with him, possibly a little oil lamp in a can with a shutter they call a dark lamp. He kept lighting it and examining the ground. But, though he passed within twenty-five yards of me, he had no luck. I had chose hard ground to walk Blacky on. An Indian with his patience might have tracked me but not Carmody. Once Carmody was so close I could hear him breathing.

Then he put out the light. He went south and his sound died off. I led Blacky carefully for an hour. Did not dare to mount him, as he was skittery after being in the cave.

We found a spring and kept near it till daylight. It was down to a trickle and drying fast. As the light got better, I heard a shot. A slug hit the dirt two yards behind. The next, fast one hit my head, face and ear from behind. I was half lying down at the time. Rolled fast behind a rock.

Blacky stood and trembled. I threw my rifle to my rear when I rolled. Then shot at a smoke ball near a rock cleft right behind me.

Carmody had his hat knocked off a few seconds later. But he had it on a stick. I counted shell and decided to let Carmody know what he faced. I watched carefully. From behind a rock I saw the dust sift down and knew he was there. The dust sifted down like flour out of a sackhole. Though I was bleeding pretty bad from the head, the blood came from the left ear, away from my sight-eye.

Opposite where Carmody was hid was a sharp point of rock shooting up straight then curled over. From in front the rock sloped in to this point. I took a double aim, so as not to let the effort spoil the shot. I aimed slow and easy first and got the hang of it. Then I dropped rifle, lay back, then picked it up for a snap-shot and hit the rock slope in the right place. That jagged rock did the work. I could hear Carmody yell first in surprise and then groan a little.

The rock piece did the work. I could hear but not see him pulling himself up the slope under cover. Then I heard the saddle squeak and then his horse hoofs dying out.

But I kept watch for a trick and nothing happened. I gave attention to my ear and face. I used the drying pool to see, as I came down. Carmody had sure spoiled my looks for life. Half the ear was torn off, as if somebody had started to sow-notch me and then had gone all the way. The flap was hanging on my cheek and had stuck there a little with the quick-dried blood. But still bleeding bad. I got an old shirt, soaked it, pressed and yelled out with the pain. But kept doing that, lying on my right side to let gravity help the blood dam up within.

This finally stopped her. I had some water to drink, ate a little dry cornmeal and pushed south, watching for Carmody. When the flap of my ear kept flopping, I tied a shirt strip around my head. I made it secure by pulling my hat down tight.

LOHMAN MEETS A STRANGER

The country here was harder riding. It was hilly in a low way, with small valleys and canyons cutting across. There was some water but mostly dry arroyos. The heat got bad.

The second noon I found shade and took a long rest. I made corn cakes, ate somewhat, and the spring was pure luck. It was the best I had struck. That low mountain water was even better than the kind up near Clayton. It had a deep, clear pool about two yards across. There was not one dead thing in it.

Grained Blacky and let him graze. Though he seemed fresh, he was still working on green stuff. I decided to grain him better just as soon as I got where I could buy some.

It was fine under the hill pines and I hated to start again. Just as I got up on Blacky, something told me to scan around. I walked back to the scrub and rock to a little rise. I was well hid and had been for all the nooning.

At first all I saw was an eagle dipping low. Then the dead sheep it was looking at. Then I heard horses walking. Two men came riding along, with one man walking. The walking man was the one I was looking for but I did not know that then. All stopped by the dead sheep and talked awhile.

Then the men on horses rode ahead to the spring I had just left. The man on foot went out of sight among rocks. I suppose he had his mount tied somewhere there.

Then I was able to see one of the mounted men sure was Carmody. It seemed to me I saw him bulge in the middle, which I had not seen before. Also his shirt front was part open and I saw white there, not the white of skin. Was sure I had slashed him.

The men were coming on far behind me, not knowing my whereabouts, I was more or less sure. The country was fair for cover and I had learned to use it. I saw them stop and examine a spring soon, though, where I had left some marks. I had tried not to.

The higher stonier ground where I might have lost them was too tough. It was so either for man or horse. After dark did not dare to fire up, or even stop.

Before the late night I got off Blacky and led him up a dry. Then started climbing.

I tied Blacky and then pulled some poor feed out of the lower rocks, hobbled him short. Kept hold of his tie-rope.

The dark was slow and thick and I had the melancholy. I had been used to having these doubts and worries for some time.

I watched their fire among the pines, and knew they were eating well. I was sure the other man besides Carmody was a Boyd or the friend or relative of a Boyd. They probably figured I had made a fireless camp on ahead and here I was behind. If this can be done, it is the best way of all to handle a situation such as I was in.

I figured her this way and knew I was right. The Boyds were sore and they were probably doing some fighting among themselves. The old man was sorest of all, and he had probably told his sons they were no account and to stay home and let his hired people fix me.

Then Old Man Boyd's hired people, I knew, were as feared of him as his sons. He had told them to act quick and get it over or worse would come. He had probably thrashed around and threatened a lot and these men, I felt, were operating with that fear behind them.

No matter how they feared Boyd, however, they did not intend to get themselves shot. No job with the Boyds or anyone is worth that. So they were driving on in a blind kind of way, showing a lot of activity, piling up a lot to report back to Old Man Boyd.

One thing I knew which was that I had this advantage strong: My father had often told me that a certain kind of Indian is hard to fight in bunches because he goes out to battle with the death-hope. He is willing or even anxious to die.

Well, I was like those Indians at this time. I was not entirely anxious to die. But I was not afraid of dying because I did not much care. The way things had gone with me and my people made me that way. So I was not afraid of death and actually wondered if I would not be happier dead.

I had not been foolishing with Bradley when I told him this. This gave me a great advantage but was no credit to me. I do not think I felt fear on the trip with one possible exception, maybe two. Once I was tarnally scared after the meet-up with the Boyd cattle. I admit that . . .

◆ ◆ ◆

Well, I saw another eagle, or maybe the same one, night-flying. This surprised me. I did not know they night-flew.

When the moon was up it came out dim. I blanketed up a little and lay back against a slant rock. In the morning I scanned up ahead of me as quickly as possible. I climbed slowly up a shale slope. Now there were four horses with the two men, so I figured they must have had visitors in the night. The hunt was heating up. They meant business.

One man was getting up the fire. I saw the one fix coffee for himself. Then, instead of calling the other, he spread his blankets and lay down. Then he sat up and began cleaning his gun. I decided at first to try to pass them and get distance ahead of them. But then decided it would be too risky. Besides, in looking for a "side door" off the trail, one side was country as open as a barn floor, the others were shale-slides mostly, too steep and tough. I would be taking a great chance of laming my horse.

Even when I started to inch down the slope where I was for watching up ahead, the shale rattled. Also I cut my hand on sharp shale trying to stop my speed and the noise.

About halfway down, I was coming down slow backwards, and there was a kink in the slope around a big rock corner. Still I was moving down backwards. Hand began to bleed bad, so stopped the far side of the rock corner and tied it up, still facing upslope. Heard a snicker, turned around. Around the rock corner, here was a little hogback going from where I stood to the rock wall. The hogback had steep sides. On the far end was a flat place that could be dropped from if a man stood at the edge of the rim above. On the hogback near this flat place was a man straddling the hogback, having slipped on me from the side. He had a knife and a gun, and my rifle was twenty yards down.

He was not more than twenty feet maybe thirty from me. I could see him plain. Lot of hair on his face.

He saw me look at my gun. He slicked out his knife and laid her flat on the palm of his hand. He smiled and looked at me with squint eyes. Every time I looked at my rifle, he'd pull his hand back. I had never seen knife throwing, was sort of curious about it and wished he would get it over with. I picked up a rock then. He put back his head and laughed. He put back the knife and I dropped the rock. He began edging to me, making it very slow. Then he came to where he could see my horse as well as my rifle, looking down.

Then he spoke the first words. "Hold dere." He looked at my horse. "Belong you?"

It sounded French-like, so I said one word, "Bawbeen."

He jumped as if shot. He stared at me. I dug out Bradley's note and threw it to him. He read it several times.

Then he said: "Amos Bradley. All right. But you want to get Santa Rosa. Not all right. Down there is a couple who will shoot the guts out of you."

We both edged down to a safe place. I picked up my rifle. He motioned me to follow him, and we both started climbing again up an easy groove I had not seen before because of a twist in the rock. We got to a flat place. It was covered with bird manure, and obviously also had been used by Indian braves. They had been sent up there for high-lonesome.

We crawled on our bellies up to the edge of the drop. The people down below had picked a bad place. We could of dropped a rock down on their heads. It was straight down. They were rolling up their bedrolls and getting their horses ready for a start. One was Carmody, the other a young man I did not know.

Bawbeen patted his rifle and looked at me. He said "Which one I shoot? Take your pick."

I thought he was joking. But he whipped up the gun and shot Carmody through the right shoulder before I could speak.

The minute it happened there was a ruckus down there. The horses jumped and pulled at their ties. Carmody yelled his head off. They must have taken an hour trying to figure where the shot came from, while Carmody got a bandage on. We stayed hidden all the time.

Finally Carmody eased up on his horse and rode back north while the other man rode south. They both thought, of course, I had fired the shot. Bawbeen thought it was funny.

-12-

MRS. BAWBEEN TAKES A HAND

From the time I met Bawbeen I didn't trust him. I may have done the man an injustice. I don't know. I felt all the time I was with him, he might throw me all of a sudden. Even when they closed in, I could not be sure he had nothing to do with it. He was a quiet man—too quiet.

All the while we watched the hullabaloo down below he never spoke. When the men lit out, he said: "You want hole up with me? Meet my wife?"

I told him sure.

We got down from the ridge. I picked up Blacky and watered him at the first spring we found. I had to pull him off for fear he would sicken himself. Bawbeen admired the horse. That was plain. He spoke of a trade and smiled.

In a gulch he had two horses tied way below where the men had camped. He got on one and led the other, loaded with the biggest traps I had ever seen. They were for wolves and bears. His horse was a buck-kneed sorrel, and must have been a hard ride. He trotted and Bawbeen jounced but he did not seem to mind.

We went up an arroyo for a ways, then hit the hill meadow where I had seen him talking to the men. A new sheep carcass was there now. It had been gutted by wolves or coyotes, some of it pretty maggoty.

I would not of touched it, but Bawbeen swore a little while. Then he rough dressed it, cutting out some of the maggoty parts.

We trailed back through the canyon, and traveled some miles till we came to a big shack. It was on a flat place with flat in front and a rise with jacks behind it and all the way down the ridge toward southwest. He had a small sheep corral, a shed or two and a broke-down wagon. He had about forty sheep. The shack was half sod, half wood, with flattened tin cans patching the roof. I heard screaming from a lean-to. Someone was in there pounding on the door.

"My wife," said Bawbeen. "I shut her up. She is sick of the wine."

All the time we were moving around, when the woman screamed Bawbeen did not seem to mind, simply repeated "She is sick of the wine."

Inside I never saw anything like that shack. There was hardly room to live, a dirty bed, a few pieces of furniture, the rest filled up with old harness, traps both good and broken, trap keys strung around, rusty pans with holes in, spiders, shovels, three saddles, two no good, two stoves besides the one he used, both broken, flea-bit wolf and horse hides and hides of other animals I didn't know. In one corner was plaits and coils of wire and old rope. There was a good deal of small-cut dried beef hanging from the rafters.

For a sink he had two wooden washtubs, one inside the other so the wore holes would not meet. Then he had bored a hole in the bottom to take the drain off. One thing, he had a good spring, plenty of water, good water.

When it got dark he opened a can of beans and made coffee. I untied Blacky and led him up the rise in a well-hid place among the jacks. I kept the blanket and surcingle on him with the rifle in the loop. Bawbeen back at the house offered me the wine jug several times but I refused. At late dark he pulled up the fire and asked me to help him in with his wife. She was sound asleep behind the lean-to door. We carried her to bed. She never even moved, a good-looking woman with dark complexion.

Bawbeen drank wine and played first the sweet potato and then the mouth organ. Then he got out a jew's harp. It was the worst music I ever heard. But he was trying to entertain me and I was polite and said I liked it, and then he would play more. Then he got a tick out of the loft for me and crawled in with his wife. I watched the fire till I fell asleep . . .

Next morning he was up early and waked me. He was standing over me with some thin copper wire and a needle. He told me he would fix my ear. I hesitated at first. Then he showed me in the looking-glass that I had rolled on my ear in sleep. It was hanging pretty bad again. I asked him why the wire, and he said "I show you—I fix."

He took a hot coal and heated the wire, then he heated the needle and washed them in hot water. Then I sat in a chair while he pierced my ear in two places and wired it up. I looked at it and the heat he had used had stopped the blood-ooze and it looked pretty good. It was snug up.

He then said nothing more and went outside while I sat to ease the burning pain and waited for Mrs. Bawbeen to wake up.

She began to roll soon and talk in her sleep. Finally she saw me, rose up and yelled things in French. But she quieted down.

I told her who I was. She asked for coffee and I brought her two cups.

She became very talkative. I asked her if she did not find it lonely. She said: "You think I live here in this dirty place? I live in town, in Santa Rosa, and come out here every so often to make sure the wolves have not eaten Henry. Did he clean last night?"

I told her I thought he had cleaned some. She looked around and said: "He has merely moved the dirt in new places."

When I asked her about the junk, she said Henry never threw anything away. He picked up junk riding around the country and brought it back and God help anyone who tried to take it from him. She found out I knew Amos Bradley and said she knew the whole family at Socorro, but the main branch was at Santa Rosa, the Spanish girls and all. She said they are "old richeros" who have lived in this country from away back. She asked me if I trusted Bawbeen. When I said yes, she said I had better not.

"The cattlemen pay him high for wolfheads and if they want you, and pay high enough, he will sell you. Do they want you?"

I said I thought they did and saw no reason not to tell her about the Boyds. I said I had my eyes peeled for the Boyds. She said I had better peel them for Henry. I hardly knew what to say.

Sitting in bed, she began to fix her hair. Bawbeen came in then and she began to talk French to him. It sounded like she was name-calling. He merely smiled at her. He said: "This our guest, so entertain." She said she would get breakfast. "Of course," said Bawbeen, "but give him his fortune with the hand."

I was puzzled by this. She got up out of bed then, when Bawbeen kept mentioning "the hand, the hand." So she came and took my hand just as Bawbeen went out when he thought he heard something. He merely mentioned hearing something and went out with no other explanation. He did everything like this.

His wife was looking at my hand. She looked and looked first at my hand, then me. Then she dropped my hand and said, "Later." She went to the sink then and threw water on her face, washed her hands, went outside for a little, then came back. She came and took my hand and then looked at me in the face. "Later," she said again. Then at the sink where she started to clean dishes, she said, "Take care, take good care," and used the Spanish term Madre de Dios. I heard her mumbling to herself, when she let me have the sink to clean up, saying Madre de Dios and French terms I knew nothing of.

I said nothing to all this, but was nervous.

Bawbeen had cut a few ribs from the uneaten sheep and they were laying on the table, half covered with a paper turned black in places with sheep blood.

She said: "You take that bloody mess out of here and tell Henry to bury it. Then stay out till I fix myself and get the place a little more like it."

I went out and gave the ribs to Bawbeen, who tied them up to hang from the eaves. He went back then to cleaning wolf traps. I gave the place a good looking at. The shack could have been placed better for protection. The sheepfold was some, and the rise of hills and rock towers behind it. I was glad Blacky was up in the pines.

Bawbeen's Colt was lying handy on a tree stump near where he had now moved his traps. I figured, if surprised, I would grab it.

Bawbeen had a little fire going, melted some cheese, mixed it with sheep fat, and kept dipping the gloves he wore into a shallow pan of fat melted with sheep blood. Then he poured this into a rusty frying pan, to cool. He cut the cheese in cubes, punched a hole in these and poured in some kind of killer from a brown bottle. Then he melted more sheep grease and plugged the holes.

Before we went in the house, he showed me a sheep shank bone and a horse shank bone cut in two like a saw had done it. He said a wolf had bit through each. I was willing to believe the sheep bone but not the horse, though my father had told me about how hard a wolf can bite, their jaw-power.

"These big wolf up from Mexico," said Bawbeen. "For each big greaser wolf I get twice as much. Greaser wolf big enough to kill cattle, mountain lion, buffalo, people, even all people in town. Magic wolf. Loup-garou."

Mrs. Bawbeen opened the door, threw out dishwater and called us in. She had cleaned up a little, but the fire was too hot for comfort. We had coffee, canned apples, sheep stew and beans. It was fair.

She ate nothing, drank coffee and abused Henry. She said he was a good bookkeeper and could work in town for the Maxwells and Springers even if he did not speak English well. She said he could write English better than speak it, and showed me French letters he had written. She said he could have a nice job, sitting at a desk in a silk shirt writing, but preferred to herd sheep. She said: "My husband is a dirty man and likes dirty work."

Bawbeen said absolutely nothing. I could see her getting angry. She jumped up suddenly and said, "This dirty son-of-a-bitching country what it is doing to this nice boy. This dirty country ruins everybody." She picked up a small knife from the stovetop and began to yell, holding the knife against Bawbeen's throat. She said: "I will cut your worthless throat, you animal, if you give this boy away to anyone. Do not do it or I will kill you sure."

Bawbeen, of course, stopped eating at this point. But he just sat and stared at the floor while the knife was at his throat. I don't believe he was scared at all. He said absolutely nothing. So then she began to scream again, taking the knife away, then coming back with more screaming.

Finally she got too tired to keep it up. She could talk no more. She sat down. Suddenly she said: "Henry is so beautiful because he is so ugly."

Bawbeen was quiet a minute. Then he took a big spoonful of beans, taking a long time to fix it, piling the beans high on the spoon. He had trouble getting them in his mouth. Then he started chewing. After chewing them he said: "Some night you will come out here again and get drunk. I will furnish the wine. Then when you are asleep I will kill you sure." He said this very quietly.

At this his wife merely laughed in a wild way.

Then she said to me and nodded: "He is right. Henry is right. He will." She seemed pleased.

Seeing the letters Bawbeen had written in French, I asked for some paper and pencil. Bawbeen had plenty of these, so gave me some, and I put down a few more tracks on paper about what I had done since leaving the Bradleys. With the hunt for me on, and not knowing how soon they would make a final hash of me, I seemed to think more and more about leaving some record of my father and me. Mrs. Bawbeen said to her husband I was writing a letter to my girl. Truth to tell I owed Restow a letter by this long time, but no way to post it.

We heard horses. Mrs. Bawbeen shoved me under the bed and pulled down the quilt. Henry went outside. But I came out from under the bed finally. I wanted to be ready for what might happen.

LOHMAN MAKES A GETAWAY

Mrs. Bawbeen finally went out and joined Bawbeen and two men who had come up. First she stayed close to the house but then moved down to the spring. Then she moved to some trees where there was a line rigged and some clothes hanging.

Not either man looked like the two I had seen the day before. They were better dressed men. The biggest was carrying a Colt when he got off his horse, but the other man drove the buckboard and was not armed though later he strapped on a gun from the buckboard.

The biggest man, with a mustache and a big scar on the back of his neck, was named Nelson. At least that is what I heard Bawbeen call him. The smaller man was tough and light and chewed tobacco and spit nervously and constantly.

They howdyed Bawbeen, who stood near his Colt on the stump and looked at them. Nelson told Bawbeen the Springers had authorized him to come and pay him for any wolfheads he had. I had a letter in my pocket from Restow for one of the Springers, but of course was impossible to use now and probably would always be.

"Wolf," said Bawbeen like a grunt. "Wolf?" He spit.

"But," Nelson said, "we want to look in your house also."

"What for?"

"Well," Nelson said, "a young polecat is drifting around the country hereabout. He might have crawled into your place last night unbeknowst to you and maybe even have died. He'll stink soon."

Mrs. Bawbeen came up then. Her dark eyes were very sad. Her hair looked fresh and tight combed where it had been oily and stringy. She shook her head. "We keep out the skunks with the fire. We keep out the big ones and the little ones, young ones and old ones. No, there is no skunk in the house, but don't go in there. It is my house and Henry's. What are you—sheriffs? Who are you to go around putting your big fat noses into private homes?"

She opened the door I was standing behind then. I could see nearly all of this, as I moved back from the bed toward the fireplace, slanting my walk and cutting my eyes toward the window. The more she opened the door, the more I slewed back.

Nelson said: "Suppose we just walk in without no asking."

"Ah fine, come, come in." Mrs. Bawbeen drew back inside the door and picked up a paring knife. She got it from the table which she had just made neat. "Come in and let me cut you up. Oh thanks, Henry, for sharpening my knife today. I will show you a large skunk with his liver cut out, like his sack."

She slammed the door in Nelson's face.

Nelson I could not see then. But could hear him laughing. The other, small man was nodding his head nervously and spitting. Inside Mrs. Bawbeen gave me a terrible frown and shove toward the bed. I hesitated and she stomped her foot, so I drifted back toward the woodbox. I sort of believed her with the knife in her hand.

Outside I heard Bawbeen say: "Good thing you not go in. She would of cut you up. My wife is terrible woman. Terrible."

The men laughed and he pulled two croker sacks out from under the house and they moved away from the door down to the spring. I could thus hear much that was going on. Mrs. Bawbeen rattled pans and kept motioning to me. I kept my eyes on the group near the spring.

Bawbeen rolled six wolfheads out of the croker sacks, two fresh and bloody. He brought a panther head from a nail. The men argued then about paying him.

Nelson showed one wolfhead had dried right down to the skull, which was true. He said it was a "relic" Bawbeen had picked up in the hills. Bawbeen did not get angry, but kept saying "Trapped him."

All the while they argued, the small man, now armed, kept watch around the place. Finally Bawbeen got sore, threw down the wolfhead that was dried and took money for the others.

The more I watched the more I liked the idea of leaving Blacky up in the jacks. But then he whinnered. Both men looked up, then at each other. The small one started for the house door. Bawbeen threw down with his Colt on the other. He said: "No shoot here. This my place."

I hightailed for the back window, as the small man reached the cabin door. Out I went. The door flew open behind me. Mrs.

Bawbeen met the small man with a shovelful of hot ash and red coals from the fire.

Even then I hoped he would not get it in the face, and he did not. His shirt was open and he got it on the bare chest, and a lot went down his shirt front. He started to scream and roll on the ground.

Under the jacks I slewed left, then up the ridge with Nelson sighting me and getting a late start. Bawbeen poured his Colt at Nelson. He threw shot after shot, but sure was weak with a hand gun. He should of had a rifle.

I never had seen such big rocks as the ones I jumped and crawled over. When I found a ledge under a lot of bush, I crawled there and watched Nelson go past.

Then when I lost sight of him I began to worry. He could move on me from behind where I was. He may have seen me, I thought. I thought he might have planned that, pretending not to see me, then doubling back.

Poked my head up from the ledge, swung by my hands to the rock above. Stopped then because I could see plenty snakes. It was one of those big families—four or maybe five coiled on ledges high above me, two down closer to the ledge I was on.

Kept my eye on them, you bet, moving carefully south in the direction of Blacky. Did not watch where I moved and dropped in a big rock gap. It had high sides, just beyond reach of my fingers. The snakes did that. I had been too busy like a fool, watching them.

Now I was in a stiff bind. I was in a rock pocket. Little hurt and shook up some. The hole was like a shallow well, but too deep for me. I looked down in the dark and could see two maybe three square feet of space to move my feet. There was a wedgy crack in the middle I was trying to stay out of. It was just the kind to get a foot wedged in.

Fixed my feet firm and made one jump to get a hand hold on the top. I could not make it. I tried several times and about wore myself out, but then catching sight of a half-dry root hanging over on the north side. I figured if I grabbed this root I might have an outside chance.

Just then I heard a snicker above. Nelson was standing on a ledge right over me. He knew he had me good. Shooting me would be like shooting a colt in a breaking box. But this was a mean man, I found out.

He could of shot right off, but he begun feeling in his pockets. Then I saw he was looking for a knife and judged he would pitch it. But this was wrong. He opened her and began hacking at a small pine, at the same time trying to twist it free.

Finally he got it half through. His belt started slipping, so he took it off with the Colt and laid it down and then twisted the tree branch free.

I had started jumping again. But then decided I had better save my strength to see what he planned. Then I saw. He started poking at the ledge below and I could see the rattler's tail over the edge. If he fell, it would be on me.

The snake fought the stick. I thought maybe Nelson was stupid, and if the snake struck enough he might have no juice left. The snake kept coiling and looping—rattle, rattle. Not wishing to leave the ledge, of course. Nelson started laughing. His laughing rose to above near-yells. I could see now he had that personality called crazy-mean. He was sweating. He was shaking all over, laughing. He yelled loudest when the snake seemed near to falling, with a big loop of him hanging over. But next recovered his hold on the ledge.

Then the stick broke. Nelson cussed a blue streak. Then he went back and wrenched off another stick. Kept laughing, working right ahead.

I began to conserve myself for a real jump at that tree root. Nelson came back and started shoving the snake again. The buzzing went on, but suddenly Nelson saw a fresh, new snake on a ledge closer to me. He made a stab at it, I yelled, the snake fell straight down past me like an arrow, landed on my feet. I stomped once but then remembered Harley stomping on a snake. The snake's head was cushioned by its own coils. Harley made no headway with it, moved once, the snake struck going in just above the shoe heel in the soft part of the shoe.

I yelled now, as the snake came down, stomped once, gave one jump and grabbed the root. Hung on and threw my feet out of the hole and up far enough to catch one heel on the ledge. Then I got leverage, rolled clear. That snake which Nelson hoped would kill me in a mean way I truly believe scared me enough in my feet to make them do the impossible.

I rolled fast into a clump of jackpines, Nelson grabbed up his gun and shot twice and missed. I rolled right into another snake that ran from me without even bothering me. Then I was up running among the trees and rocks.

I could hear Nelson thrashing around in the hillside brush, cussing behind me. I pushed ahead for where Blacky was hid. Once I thought I had found the place and thought he was stole. But I had the wrong spot, turned around and looked up instead of down. There was his shiny hind end sticking out from behind the trees.

Just as I got on and slid my rifle out of the loop, Nelson came on me from one side. He started toward me, did not see the rifle on my right, as I was facing upslope. He picked up a rock to heave. He had his gun in his left hand. It was the first time I ever started a snapshot without too much thinking. Swerved the gun to my left, then hesitated and the gun spoke for itself as Nelson heaved the rock. The shot was nearly a clean mistake, but the slug hit him square on the forehead and he died, went down like a tree, never moving.

Nelson fell down between a couple of fallen trees, face up looking at nothing with open eyes. It was scary. From where I sat my horse, he looked like a man in a coffin betwixt those trees. The pines, taller here lower down, were like a church with Nelson in a coffin.

I felt scared. Sitting there on Blacky, I knew my doom was sealed. Or had come closer. I had not meant to kill the man, just stop him. That trigger of my rifle I had filed too much—too hairline for safe. Good for speed. But I knew I had to dull down that trigger. I had shot with hardly aiming. Such things will happen once in a lifetime.

Blacky was cut with a sharp rock just above the foreleg. Nelson had some revenge. It is a bad muscular place to wound a horse. He was bleeding.

Starting to get off, I thought of myself and my own worries. There might be others in the vicinity besides the man I had shot and his friend back with the Bawbeens, by now not in the best of shape with a chest full of burned places. I had seen many more men since leaving the Bradleys than I honestly thought the Boyds would send against me.

I threw out the spent shell and wiped the stock. I wanted to throw the rifle away for just a minute. I sat looking at the gun. That gun I knew I could never throw away. I remembered then how I had come by it. Nevin, before his death, had owned a Winchester and had taken me on a chuck wagon circuit to find a man he was supposed to arrest, working with the O Bar Y outfit.

At night we caught up with the wagon and the man had vamoosed. But we spent the night with the cowpokers. Nevin's Winchester was bright-new then and he cared for it like a little baby. He had it in a heavy, fringed rifle-boot, but some careless person had nudged it up to the fire so that the muzzle heated up close to red hot. Nevin found the gun in this condition and almost went crazy, throwing the rifle in the brush.

He would never look at the gun again and I got it and hid it from him. Then I took it to a man who knew guns and he sawed the muzzle down, losing less than a half inch, and now it was my gun. All this came over me, as I looked at my gun, thinking what I should do about fixing the trigger. I drew in the pine smell to steady myself like a man will take a whiskey shot. Blacky stomped in the fresh manure around him and kept turning his head to see his wound.

Nelson was lying there face up. He sure had been a damn fool.

I turned down the rock slope and when I saw the back of the Bawbeen place I swerved left and came out from the jackpines a half mile below the house. Maybe further but I could see what was going on.

There was a gully further down and I ducked into this, threw the lines over the horse's head and found him some grass to let him chew and slaver. I got some slaver and rubbed it on the wound and he slavered it some more with his mouth while I shinned a tree to see the Bawbeens.

Bawbeen had the scrawny man on his back in the buckboard and seemed to be larding his chest out of a can. I would of done the same. The missus was at the door watching.

I clomb down and walked Blacky south across the meadow, keeping a little ways up the slope under the pines, till I was away. Then mounted and rode south. I decided there would be no more fooling. There would be no more skulking around and I would hit for Socorro fast.

At near noon rested the horse, got out Amos's map and studied her. I had troubled the Bawbeens and now decided I would not hook up or bed with anyone, at least no man with wife and house. The map was sweaty and dirty but still readable. I thought I would ride fast to the north pass which was T Harris Canyon, cross through the gap and head down straight for Socorro. Before me I had the Sandios range and that put me near the edge of the Estacia Valley. The valley was broad and dry, mostly dry grass, horse-belly high in places. Amos had told me the Apaches had burnt it off some further down from where I was.

Though open country, I decided to cross the valley right from where I was, and hug the Sandios on the way down, watching for hill trickles to the east. I figured on pushing Blacky—push him a half hour and five minutes rest, then a longer rest every two hours, possibly at water. I shortened the work periods and stretched the rest periods some.

The map I folded up and pushed in the grain sack to dry a little, got on my horse and pushed. Once or twice Blacky favored his cut leg, but I watched that carefully. In a young horse the heat of travel sometimes speeds up the healing. To my impatient mind seemed I could cross the valley in one big drive, but it seemed long, because of many rests. Also I watched the back trail. I was sure it would be one man or two men, as usual.

About sundown the mountains got really close. I stopped for rest, then saw a hill trickle I went for, one of those I had been seeking. Then I saw two men top a rise, see me, stop and start to backtrack. It was coming on gray then with a higher wind, thick dust in bare spots and the prettiness of twilight in the dividing line of foothills. I started a trash fire to show I did not care, but watching close.

Sun had about an inch to fall behind the Sandios when I boiled the coffee and got it down to keep me awake all night. Blacky was grassed light and had another sip. I stomped out my fire and turned south in the near dark. The cold wind started blowing north to south on my tail, which helped after the after-noon cooking of me and my horse in the broad places. Now in the rest periods I thought I heard hoofs.

Amos had said: "They'll cheat, so watch out. They don't want none of that rifle."

One of the men following me could have been the one with Nel-son but I doubted that with his chest hurts. Could not be Carmody. Must be two new men. It looked as though by now the Boyds were building a big hunt across states. Easy for the Boyds to do this, with these cattle clubs being formed. All were fighting rustlers, some even the sheep-herders, which was why I thought Bawbeen had been smart to protect himself by killing wolves for cattlemen.

Blacky started to slow and worry the bit. Two hours after sun-down I grassed and grained him light. At a trickle in the rock wall I watered him under the shelter of a ledge. Was there too long, for I heard a rock slide start above, and then a rock hit me on the head and nearly knocked me down. I heard a laugh.

Quick as I could I hauled Blacky under the ledge and sat under him while a cylinder full of hand-gun fire chipped off bits of the ledge. It was more calculated to work on my nerves as they knew they had as much chance of hitting me in the blowy dark as a centipede or a plains lizard. Still it was a try.

I knew better than to move. So sat still and worked it out. The other man was possibly back with their horses, or out near me waiting for me to be scared out by the pistol. But they were stupid, for I listened and could hear the one above going back among the rocks. So mounted quietly and rode ahead.

Decided they now wanted me in the canyon. We made T Harris Canyon an hour before midnight and did its 22 miles as the final dash to the Grande Valley in about two hours prior to sunup.

Now Blacky was plain fagged. I took off my shirt and hand rubbed him in the most soothing places. I led-walked him a little. Waited and rested a long time.

Just as the dawn began to get its dim light, I walked up a rise and gave the country a careful view. Blacky was not going good. The men were not to be seen, but there was a movement to the south and I could make out very dim a Mex and a burro coming up in that direction.

I turned west then, and as we came out of the canyon and topped the rise where the land began to tilt the other way, it grew dark again in the shadow of the mountain. Found a little water further down. Heaviest flow was shoulder-high, so I filled the can, then filled my hat with my finger through the peak hole and Blacky spilled some of this but got most of it.

-14-

THE TRAIL SOUTH

On ahead of me in the dark, with the mountains now behind me, I could almost feel the Grande. The trail divided at the end of the canyon. One went north for a little, stopped and ended in nothing, which I found out. The other piece went south along the base of the hills. I was taking my time about planning and finally headed south slow along this trail. I thought I would rest till light, even though I had been going slow a long time. After light, I thought, I would make the crossing of the mesa that lay between me and the river in early gray. Was unsure of the country from here on and wanted to know.

We ambled slow ahead in the dark. I kept listening for sounds of mounts behind. We came to a spring and I offered water to the horse but he refused. Then I heard sounds behind and pulled back fast and turned into a clove place in the rise. Blacky did not make a sound. We waited and soon it proved to be the Mex with the burro, going along slow and easy in the dark.

We stayed there till he was out of sight, then come up behind him. A side trail back into the rise opened up. I decided to stay here till light. I hobbled the horse and sat down and watched for what I had heard about—these New Mexico sunrises. The sun now must be near the mountain-tops behind me. I had been fooling around too long at the head of T Harris Canyon.

When it got brighter there was a sound behind and above me on the trail. I looked up there and there was the burro munching grass, with the Mex sleeping against a tree trunk, with the lead rope noosed over one of his feet. I could see his shoe soles. Both had holes in them and his serape was muffled up so high you could hardly see his head. I paid him no mind.

Now it got light enough so that I could see if I rode straight ahead I would surely strike the Grande, and the north-south road from Santa Fe to Socorro.

The land this side of the mountains seemed bigger than the other side. As the sun got higher up, the flat, dry slope to the west down to the river looked like a gold country in the early, soft shadows. In the first light you could see every grass blade distinct. From where I sat I could even see insects lightering up and down the grass blades.

The early wind would blow down the little gulches and make the grass wave in places like Mex women dancing. Now that the sun was rimming up behind me, there were streaks of light and dark that were pretty as could be. The small winds kept blowing, then bigger, general winds would come. The whole grassland bowed to the wind and came back with a salute.

Still I was waiting for those men. Still they did not show. I was not anxious to be a plain target for them on that flat mesa grass to the river, with them spotting me from the high up. Yet I wanted no more travel in the dark now till I hit the river. The river would be reliable. So for half hour or so I rode short pieces down the road edge of the slope, due south, rifle out, waiting.

I found a dry that was deep but passable, hightailed down there due west for several miles and come out on the level where I thought I saw the Grande shining in the distance. But was wrong. This was just a small lake, half dry, just a dip in the land filled with water.

There was poor cottonwoods there and poor pines. But I got up one of them and scanned around and could see a bigger strip of cottonwoods north to south along the east bank and also could actually see the river.

Then back from the tree I scanned and there they were. They were leached onto me all right. They had stopped for a breakfast fire right near where I had stopped mile and a half east of the lake. I had started to fire up there, then decided against it, and they saw my tracks and brush. I could even see in the early clear the glint of the metal above the holsters, and the shine of their wore-handled frying pan and the horsehair smoke. I got hungry watching, so watered Blacky at the lake, got a drink for myself, chewed dry bacon and was ready for them. I swung up. Blacky now felt rested and good and we made the river in less than expected time. They were out of sight then.

Now I hit the trail to Socorro right along the river. It was good plain road, heavy tracked. There was a gully down the stream which was the outflow point of the same arroyo I had used for cover miles back, showing how I had ridden a near straight line to the river. I pulled the horse halfway down the arroyo, careful for sudden water though there was no sign of a drench as far as I could see to east. I also wanted to be careful not to get dry-gulched. Here it would be the real thing.

Just was getting ready to lift river water in my can, to pour into my hat, when saw this dust cloud to the north and heard the wheel-creak. The creak was loud enough signal for anybody. I believe you could of heard it for miles like an owl scritch. I moved to the middle of the road carefully, then saw a two-mule, four-horse team with a freighter and a smaller wagon hooked behind. The mules were wheelers.

I saw who was driving and raised my hand. He pulled up with a lot of heavy cursing at the off lead which was shying at a dead gopher snake.

It was Jake Leffertfinger, the freighter man I had talked to in Twist about my father. He asked where I was going. I said I was acting on his advice in the saloon that day.

He said: "Bub, turn back, they is a big drive on for you. I heard it twice up the road a piece. Turn back."

I told him I could not do that.

For a long time he said nothing, just looked at me. Then he said: "Won't go back, huh. Positive?"

I said yes.

Then he sat looking at me a long time again. "Very well," he said, "then if you wish to have it that way, we will arrange for some protection for you." I told him quickly about the men behind me, saying I did not want to tangle him.

"Oh you don't," he said. He looked at me while he got down from the wagon and began to fumble in behind under the canvas. He kept glancing my way and fumbling. He found what he wanted evidently, then turned.

"You skeered?"

I said no.

"Do I look skeered?"

I said no.

"Are you implying that you are not skeered but I am skeered?"

I said no.

"All right," he said then, "we will arrange for your protection." He brought out a shotgun, a carbine, two Colt pistols and a couple of boxes of shell and laid them prominent on the wagon seat. "There," he said, "that will surely astonish them. That will warn them good. My God I was the cause of all this my God. Tie your horse to the tailpiece and sit up here with me. We will proceed to Socorro, having, with your gun, four others to work in possible need."

As I did as was bid, I felt for the first time I need not jump at every shadow. We looked for the men behind, but saw no one. We were about to start when the wheel gave a yell which reminded Jake. He wiped the short gray hairs all over his red face with a big blue handkerchief, took off his hat, put it on. He wiped his face again and gave his throat a good wipe where his Adam's apple kept twitching up and down. He seemed embarrassed.

"This war-whoop wheel of mine—this turkey caller. Mind if I ask you to help me grease her before we start."

I said no, of course, and we jacked the wagon with a hinged brace which is two short thick planks hinged together. You set them on the ground wide under the axle and tap their bases toward each other with a sledge. We took off the wheel and greased the axle and she ran fine from there on.

Twice I saw dust blowing up toward us from behind through the long grass, but did not heed much. Jake gave me some cold bacon and bread and I ate as we ambled on. We did not talk much except now and then Jake would say he was disappointed in my friends. I referred to the wagons being empty. Jake said: "I did not wish to slouch around for a load. They's been another silver strike at Magdalena. Fetch and carry for a while down there. I would like for you to admire my mules. They are scarce and dear, smarter than a horse and work on anything. These ones this morning had a handful of cactus pods and some leather shoelaces I don't need any more."

Once in a while he would mention my father and counsel me against going on. He told me he had thought of something which might mean that the Boyds would hit at my father to spite me. He used this as an argument, but I said I thought it was all the more reason I should join my father. But he seemed to hate the Boyds. "The family think they are made of special clay."

We joked a lot. I spoke once about Jake being red-haired and his name which did not seem to jibe. He just laughed. "I've wore hats that never fit, also. This name of mine was the one lying around loose, so I put her on to keep the sun off." My father had often spoke to me about the country being full of men with changed names.

Toward midafternoon I looked back and there they were and told Jake. He looked around the top-frame quick and looked long, with the mules still ambling along behind the horses. Then he pulled up fast, jammed the brake and twisted up the lines on the brake bar. He stood up in the seat, and first shot off the shotgun and reloaded her, then the rifle, then a couple shots each from the pistols. The men behind had stopped, when the wagons stopped. It was strange to watch Jake.

He sat down again, reloaded where need was, and started the team again. The wagon moved and the men came on slow. "You understand," Jake said, "I want them to know we have what-for to shoot with. You understand these hired men are likely to be a little bit stupid, so it is just as well to make it plain as pie. Some of them don't even understand clear English."

We kept on going. Now the men caught up with us. They took their time passing us, acting as if we were not there. Not even a howdy. But they took in everything and seemed a little nervous. One of them twitched a little when Jake asked me in a loud voice if I would please keep him from shooting people. Said he was an alligator and ate people. He said he was a terror on wheels and had a crazy itch to shoot any human thing he saw. He said he hoped I would not let him shoot anybody, as he was terrible when he got started. "I'm a heller," he said.

The men heard, of course, but paid no mind. They kept their faces straight ahead. One was an ordinary Texas type, smooth-faced, about ten years older than me. The other was a tough-looking man with a left leg cut off at the knee, so that he bore down rather heavy on the off stirrup. His gun sheath was cut off like his leg and had a shotgun in it.

At a notch in the Grande shore when Jake hauled up the team for a drink, he said: "First time I ever been followed by people in front of me."

The sun got hotter towards noon. It seemed even hotter in middle afternoon. At dark the land seemed to have trouble cooling off.

Jake saw my sunburned hands, and the left with the slight hole in it from my long dry walk up north. He told me some stories on himself about sunburn. Then one to laugh at about the man who got his bald head so burned that when he put on his wig it caught fire.

We camped early and took sleeping turns. When it got light the men ahead were getting their breakfast fire started. They then grained their mounts after instead of before, showing they were no good.

"They will never do a thing to us," Jake said. "They haven't the guts. No sir."

I was not so sure.

Jake said he was thinking of a plan and would tell me about it when he had had time to give it more brain power.

Before noon of the next day we passed the Ladrone Mountain on the Grande's west bank. Jake said the mountain was made entirely of colored rocks and crystal stuff. He said robbers had once hidden there and I might like to try it. I saw once again Jake was getting doubtful of the idea of getting me to Socorro.

The two men up ahead of us were moseying right along. It had gotten so we paid little attention to them and it seemed they had forgotten us. Jake said the part he hated about this was the bold way they did it. But his mind was mostly on my father.

After thinking awhile he said maybe it would be better for me to "collect" my father, as he put it, and get him further south for his health. He was not making a joke about this. He suggested Magdalena and offered to ride us over.

We got to talking and he gave me more information about my father. "He is working for this T Cross T outfit owned by a Britisher. They have been under the eye of the law but most people down this way think this is silly. They may have fooled some with hair-branded calfs. As for your father, his past as a peace officer is known and no one would possibly suspect him of lifting cows. He would not steal the pried-up corn off a man's small toe. But the trouble with T Cross T, they have a couple of former rustlers with them, Steven Martin and Bud Gallatin. The Britisher, Gerard, knows this and has been warned about it but seems plain stubborn about it. The last I heard the T Cross T was camped north of Socorro, having some work to do with cattle inspectors. It was said more or less that if Gerard did not clean up his bunch, some hotheads some night would naturally ride out there and shoot some folks."

In the morning of that day the off lead horse which Jake said was poor-shod picked up a sharp stone twice and the second time we had a bleeder. Jake tarred up the hoof and I called his attention to sharp rock on the trail. While we worked on the horse the two hired men ahead watched. I told Jake: "They are emptying a sackful of shale they got up on the slopes." Jake said nothing but when towards noon the shale appeared again and the men lagged, Jake drew up the team suddenly, rose up and started yelling and began firing off his Colt in the air.

Jake called them all the names he could think of. They just stopped, sat their horses and stared at him. So we started again.

All that afternoon and the morning of this next day the air was full of fine dust blown up at us by a wind from the south. Jake said it was blowing up from some dry beds further south along the Grande.

We had put handkerchiefs over our faces tied in the back, and the men up ahead of us had done the same thing. The dust kept blowing all late afternoon and was still in the air next morning. It was in the cans and frying pans and food.

The face handkerchiefs gave Jake the idea.

Along about noon of that day we came to a little dobe house neat-made, with sheds in the back, and a fine horse trough. The name of the people was Hoffman. Jake knew them well.

The husband that Jake wanted to see was off in Santa Rosa. But Mrs. Hoffman, who was considerable crippled with rheumatism, was with her son, Edward.

We had some coffee in their kitchen, Jake passing the time of day with Mrs. Hoffman. Ed, the son, was about 24, shaped like me, tall and about the same weight. He had wanted to go to Socorro on business but was waiting until his father got back from Santa Rosa, so as not to leave his mother alone.

He would take my place on Blacky or sit in the seat with Jake and lead Blacky just as I had done, and I would stay at the place and follow on to Socorro in a day or so on Ed's horse, which he said he had in his stable.

Mrs. Hoffman was out of the room and asleep when Jake told us this idea. Ed thought it over carefully, as it was a good way for him to get to Socorro fast. But I would not make the change unless I felt it would be safe for Ed.

Ed at this point seemed to think I was doubting his courage, which of course had nothing to do with it. He looked at me rather disgusted, went to the parlor and came back with a Colt and belt buckled on. "Come on," was all he said.

With a handkerchief over his face, Ed looked enough like me to make it good. It was agreed Ed and I should make the change-back of horses a few days later if possible at Reamer's Livery Barn in Socorro. Still I did not like it for Ed's sake, but did not like to press the matter as it began to look as if maybe Jake was getting nervous at having me with him.

We all looked out the window and saw the two men down the road keeping watch of the house, grassing their horses in an open field of the Hoffmans, which made Ed mad. So we said goodbyes.

I found out from Ed later the following week that the men did not find out about the switch until the next morning several miles this side of Socorro, after all had ridden all night pushing fast. Ed rode right past them deliberately and laughed in their faces. They stopped, had a powwow and started back galloping toward the Hoffmans, now many miles, about 35 to 40, behind.

After Ed and Jake had left, Mrs. Hoffman slept but woke about sundown.

I explained in a kindly way. It was plain she did not like it at all. I tried to make it up to her by making several cups of tea for her at her request. Then I washed the dishes and brought in stove wood. Having once said her say, she would not speak again and retired early.

-15-

THE TOOL-SHED DOOR

At first I had decided to wait for Mr. Hoffman to get home. We had agreed on that plan so his wife would not be alone on the place. Hoffman was expected to arrive the next morning early.

I found a lantern after while, went to the shed, found Ed's bay there, about the same size as Blacky but older. Tied him on the far side of the house to a mailbox post near some box elder. Then I went back to the house and sat in the rocking chair near the window all night and was there when dawn came up.

I could see the yard plain. There was a wooden windmill Hoffman had started to build to pump water. In this he had been unsuccessful and the windmill was unfinished. Just beyond this windmill I could see the hand-fed horse trough and two sheds, one for tools, one for horses.

The tool-shed door, when morning came, was half open and blowing easy in the wind. It would blow wide open, then come back slow, but never quite enough to close all the way. I begun to think someone was inside the shed. Could not see this, but could feel it.

I was sure the two men following us had gone on ahead with Ed and Jake, but one of them could have doubled back. But this was not likely as Jake and Ed would of warned me. So it was someone else.

As I watched the door swing my eyes got tired, strained and watery. I looked away to ease them, then back. Door still swinging in the wind.

I looked away again, and then back and the door was still swinging, first big swings and then smaller and smaller.

Tried watching the door from sideways to ease my eyes.

At that point the door swung to further than ever before. Someone inside had been waiting for that. A hand and arm came out and pulled the door full shut, possibly hooking it on the inside. It was fast shut from then on. It blew in the wind no more.

My stomach felt small and cold. I wondered where this man had come from. I had seen no horse, heard nothing. But one thing was sure—Mrs. Hoffman and I were not alone on the place.

I had Ed's bay tied on the offside of the house from the sheds. It was near a cleared place for wagons and a box-elder strip.

I eased out of the rocking chair and crossed the room to the other window in the direction of this locality. I eased up the window and got out. It took me two jumps to get to that bay of Ed's and get to hell out of there.

I ran the bay to northwards where I had come from. Then saw a near hill and walked him up to scan the Hoffman place from that point. All was peaceful. Not a soul in sight. The shed door was still closed.

Somehow I could not understand this. If a man had been in the shed, and I was sure he was, he would of heard me ride off and followed.

The light got better as the sun rose up. I sat my horse there a long time on the hill among the trees. I moved back, tied the bay and ate some bread and meat that Ed had fixed for me along with other food in the bags. Ate very little, knowing now that the time might be long for me through unknown country.

As I was finishing the stuff, I heard horses on the north-south road and got up quick to scan the Hoffman place. Two men on horses rode into the Hoffman yard. They were men I had never seen before, but must have been part of the hunt.

The door to the shed opened and out came Mrs. Hoffman and I almost fell over. Here I thought she was in bed and it had been her in the shed all the time. She must have been afraid of me, I figured. Had locked herself in the shed all night, probably dozed some, then the wind suction had unhooked the door. So she tried to close it without being seen.

She must have seen me leave the place through a crack or some place, because the men did not search the premises. Or maybe she did not tell on me, though fearing me. The men rode on south towards Socorro.

Yet I knew they would do this, if they figured I was near and somewhere high up watching them. So I was not fooled by this, knowing they were planning to cut back fast, or might have been.

I hardly moved that day, which was beautiful, no more blowing dust as before, the sun not too hot, and pleasant, gentle wind. I stayed close, being able to see the Socorro road north and south for quite a ways. In all that day nothing moved on the road north or south.

When it came dark, I decided to chance it, got the bay untied and led him down to the road, mounted and five shots popped near me. One tore off my old hat and sent her sailing away in the dark for good.

Ed's horse was not broke for gunfire, and he ran off to the right at top speed and carried me across the flat down to the Grande before I could stop him. Stopped him near the river, but this was flat, tilted, mesa country without a lick of cover.

I regretted the loss of my old hat, and wondered if this hunt might go on till I was a naked man riding a horse. My pants and shirt were near rags and my shoes had no soles. The old ideas came back about how these Boyds grudged me everything. Once I had seen a man, a fugitive like me, brought out from the plains by my father. I recollected how he looked—nearly naked, half crazy and looking like an animal. I saw that coming for me.

But I forced these ideas away.

Finally I got on the hill side of the road, away from the river, by slow-walking. I stopped to muffle the horse's feet with long grass and old calftag twine. Thus had a shock. Both saddlebags containing the food Ed got for me and some Jake had thrown in were off in the bay's bolt across the flat. Ed had slighted the pack straps. Right off I began to feel hungry. . . .

The next seven days I don't recollect so well, except I kept plugging on to reach Socorro. I stayed always in the hills, taking trail wherever I could find it, which was not often. When there was no trail I kept slogging south on anything Ed's horse could hold onto with his feet. The bay had green food and there was plenty water, but it was hard for me to find anything to eat.

My father often had told me how hard it seems to find game when a man is in deep need for it. A deer would of helped but I saw no deer. I ate a dead fish one night I found by the river shore and one day trailed a sheep, not wild but stray, private-owned. Followed that sheep all day but could not get near enough for a shot which I would of chanced being pretty weak.

Even watched for beaver and rats in the river but saw none. Found a cache with food all eaten by animals, except some bread which was unfit to eat but I got it down. Also shot and tried to eat some small animals I would rather not mention.

Once at about last light of day I saw a small duck in the river, when I had crawled that way through dense cover. I knocked him out with a stone. Had trouble with the feathers but finally skun him and cooked him as well as I could late at night. He was the poorest eating duck I ever saw, one of these small, skittering ducks.

I got thin and thinner, hogging water aplenty to keep the cramps down. It sure was a poor, sorry country for man and beast, sure was. . . .

I came to Socorro early Saturday morning when the town was asleep and not a soul in sight. I circled the town once. But now I was mean and desperate enough to hate myself for having skulked all these days. I looked over my rifle and decided I would shoot the first man I saw who looked as if he might be looking for me. Now I was through skulking and was mean and anxious to meet this man whoever he might be. (This changed attitude in me came out stronger later.)

Jake had described the main saloon to me and it was easy for me to pick her out. I rode down there. There was a big door in front six men could have rode abreast through. There was two back doors, one open, one cross-boarded and nailed shut. It was a well-built place, half dobe half frame. Jake had said there was a redhead bartender in the place. I heard whistling as I tied up to the hitch rail. I walked in. The redhead bartender was there all right, washing glasses, whistling, all alone.

I had never before seen a bartender wearing a white vest. He looked at me and my gun and asked me if I had seen any deer. I told him I had not but had looked for some. He said deer were getting scarce, something I could of told him. He asked me if I would not sit down. I took a chair and told him I was the son of a man he might have heard of—Mr. Charles Lohman.

When he heard this he stopped his work behind the bar and wiped his hands. He then shifted his specks and folded his arms on the bar and looked at me.

I asked him if he knew my father and he said he knew him very well. He said my father had been in his place just the day before and was now to the best of his knowledge at a T Cross T camp in a cottonwood grove about four miles above town on the Santa Fé road.

He saw then something was wrong with me. When I asked him for food and showed him money to buy it, he told me to wait and he would go out back. He seemed to have living quarters back there, but when he came back with the food, I was sure he had also sent some message. I felt this.

On a plate he had three hard-boiled eggs, and some bread. Also he had a piece of cheese on the plate and a half a dozen tortillas.

He said he was sorry he did not have hot food but had not started a fire in his stove yet. I stuffed the tortillas in my shirt, ate the rest of the food as slow as I was able, and asked for a glass of water after paying.

THE HELL BENT KID 113

It took me a long time to get the food down, as I was careful. I sat there facing the bartender at a card-table chair, with my rifle in my left arm crook, eating with my right hand from the plate. The bartender tried to go on with his work, but I could see he was so interested he could not keep his mind on it. He had a very good personality.

I asked him if my father and the T Cross T had been up north of the town a long time.

He said: "Three weeks. They were camped further north before that. They are having some difficulty with the cattle inspectors. They say they will begin the drive-out next week, but I wouldn't know. When your father was here yesterday someone brought him a letter from up north saying you were coming here. So you are the boy, are you?"

I said yes.

I was surprised some when he said: "There is another son here."

I asked the name and he said he thought the name of the other son was Harley, but could not be sure, and this surprised me even more. We had not heard from Harley for long.

He said Harley had come up from Mexico. Knowing how my father had grieved at Harley's absence, I was glad to know they had gotten in touch again. I asked was my father still cooking for the outfit. The bartender said yes. I said I had been away from my father a long time and had worried about his health.

He kept quiet then but finally said: "Probably other things."

I said something about cattle.

"Well," he said, "it's these protective clubs they form that contain the hotheads and the big mouths. The Springers and Maxwells are interested, and so are the Leffermans and other ranchers south and east of here. But the real tough guys with the shooting itch are these Boyds who are spreading down this way, or would like to."

I thanked him kindly.

A short, heavy-built man about fifty with a toothpick in his mouth came in and looked at me. I just sat there. He walked back and forth looking at me and I saw the badge on him.

"Expecting somebody?"

I said: "I have got kind of used to expecting somebody."

"But not me."

The bartender said, "This is the son of Charles Edward Lohman."

"Oh," said the man, looking at me and moving his toothpick around in his mouth.

After a little he said: "Okay, Son, get on your way. Keep the shooting out of the city limits."

I said nothing, but went out, after cocking my rifle. I then got on my horse and rode northwards without seeing anyone. It appeared to me whoever was watching wanted to make it easy for me to reach my destination.

-16-

LOHMAN FINDS HIS FATHER

The cottonwoods were thick here, not strung out along the river. They had the same musty smell as the river ones. There was a dead sheep that made me recollect Bawbeen when I got off my borrowed horse. It was lying half in the light brush at the edge of the grove, and plenty coyotes had been at it. Knowing the ways of my father and the men with him, I wondered why they had left something like that so near camp.

It made me believe they had possibly been in the habit of coming on the camp from upriver, instead of where I rode in, and had not noted the sheep. I examined the head, which was whole and near fresh, backing up the idea.

There was a path into the place. The next I noted was a tent stake and a torn-up canvas fly, like the kind of a cook's fly that is attached to a chuck wagon. Then there was a cleared space and the ashes of two fires, and it looked as if camp had been broken sudden.

Trying to see everything in front of me, as I went ahead, this made me careless of what was above. Something parted my hair. I looked up and was surprised to see it was a hanging man. His boot had parted my hair. It rose up when I saw another man hanging, then one more, which was my father.

I sat down on a log. There was no mistake. The knot on the far side was pushing his head way over. The face was in poor shape, and I think I knew him to be my father because of the baldness, mustache and crooked small, left finger. For a full two minutes I shook all over.

After some time I went back and got on my horse and rode up the Grande a ways. I think already I was looking for someone to kill, but saw no one which was surprising in a way and in another way not. The shock was bad, but believe I thought if I went away and came back, the hanging men might not be there. That it had been a mistake or dream, but when I came back they were there all right.

Began to feel cold, but recognized it as a strong and not a weak feeling. I had been weak when I went to that saloon, but too much had happened since to make me even think of that. My stomach was like a cinch knot. I realized then I should have gone with my father when he crossed the state line and not stayed at Restow's.

After I got out on the limb, where I had seen the rope's shortness, I lashed the saddle rope that I went back for, into a slip knot on the hanging rope. This knot would squeeze tight. So when I cut the other with my knife, I could ease the body down slow.

This was successful, so I began looking for a flat, sharp stone, found none, but found a half-rusted spade with no handle. The digging in that ground was tough work. The spade was rusted, it kept breaking off at the bad side, so when I got through, it was like a knife not a spade. But I got quite a good grave dug. If there had been time I would have liked to pick a better place.

After I had got the place decently covered, I stoned the top, then began to consider the two other men, as it did not seem fair to ignore them as they probably had been friends with my father. One was about as old as my father, the other young, with a good frame, and bare feet that looked as if they had been burned.

In digging around I was concentrating hard on the hard ground, so the first touch on my right ear I thought was a bug and flicked at it with my hand, which came in contact with the end of a rifle. Quickly I swung to left and then right and back, so that I was now kneeling back on my rear, looking at a man who stood covering me with a Winchester somewhat like mine. He was about my build, only with heavier shoulders, judge about 10 pounds heavier, 28 or 30. He had a mean face, whole face thin, nose curved, jawline curved like two rib bones, thin mouth.

He said: "What are you up to?"

I told him.

"These men mean anything to you?"

I told him that they did somewhat. It was beginning to feel strange to me that this man did not know how I felt, and thought he had all the advantage merely because he was holding a rifle on me. I might have respected that condition at other times but not now. That rifle meant nothing to me the way my mind was working.

He kept me covered, spit out a chew and took a fresh one from his shirt pocket. I could of handled him then, but was so confident because of an unfamiliar feeling inside of me that I let it go and waited. I have thought this matter over a good deal since and believe for all purposes I had gone insane for the time.

He spit tobacco juice, looked at me and smiled.

He said: "What's the matter with you, Bub, you scared?"

I said and did nothing.

He shifted his rifle, moved back, keeping me covered. He unbuttoned his pants and urinated on the grave. He was smiling at me all the time he did this, fixed himself, moved back towards me, and, as I expected, moved a little too close.

My mind was blurring but I tried hard to keep hold of my reason. He shot once when my left hand reached out and held the muzzle, and the slug hit the ground three feet behind me, and, of course, he could not reload. I held the muzzle to the ground and broke his wrist with my right foot, as I kicked the gun from under his hand and under his shoulder. He did not have time to strike even one blow, and I do not believe he uttered a sound. I knocked him to the left with my right fist, and again to the right with my left, the blows landing good and solid, kicked him square in the face when he was down, jerked him up by the broke wrist, so that I could feel the split, green bone grind under my hand. He made a sound then, one big scream.

I kicked him several times when he fell then, jerked him up and clasped him around the legs with my arms at the knees, for he was helpless, flopping by this time, but this made no differ-ence to me, and, holding him off his feet in my clasped hands and arms I ran him back against a tree, using his head for a hammer against the tree, snapping his head back against the tree trunk, till I thought I would knock out his brains. I let go then and his body slumped down over my head like a cape. I reached up and threw him away.

He was still breathing, and it angered me to see it. I picked up his rifle but dirt had made it dangerous to use and I ran back to my horse and my own rifle. I ran all the way back to the grove then, and just as I reached the clear with my rifle to finish him off with a shot, three men who had been running from the opposite direction, came in at the opposite side and stared at me.

I swung the sight on them and yelled to them not to move. They became motionless and frozen. I think this was surprise as much as fear. One of them started toward me, but stopped when I yelled.

People who hear about this will not perhaps believe that I was deaf with hate. I have heard of this happening to people, that some senses can leave you. It shocked me for a little to realize I had yelled and not heard the sound of my own voice. I do not apologize for this hate, for I had been sore tried.

The men were putting up their hands, without anyone ordering them to. This was when the fear began to operate on them as they saw I was out of my mind, because I sure did act that way and believe I was.

I laughed at their hands going up and told them to stop being foolish, to bring their hands down quick and unbuckle their belts. One was not armed at all, but the other two belts came down and one man had trouble because his pants kept sliding down. He stood there trying to hold them up by bowing his legs. He put his hand to his waistband at the side once and I snapped a shot through his hand. He tried it no more, but held up his bleeding hand, shaking his head at me. Then he held up both hands clasped over his head and fell on his knees and started to pray. He may have felt like the others that I was holding back from shooting them all. It is strange how men who think they are tough can break and soften up quick, and this applied to all three of them.

I looked at the man on the ground then. I wanted to cut him to ribbons, club him up final. Shooting was too easy. I think this effort of mine to find a way to pay them off slowed me and calmed me down somewhat. Furthermore controlling the three men helped me think and I had not thought for some minutes.

But I was still acting on impulse some for when one of them said in a low voice, "It's the Lohman kid—" I snapped a shot at him without thinking and knocked off his hat and put a permanent crease, lifelong, in his hair. Hitting them at short range like this sickened me gradually, it was so easy. Like bull's-eye shooting in a testing vise. Could hardly miss.

I backed off. I reached down with my left hand and unbuckled the dying man's belt, and put it on with the holster and gun. I do not know how I did this without losing the throwdown. I do not know this right up to now. But it seemed easy to do at the time.

The three men's names were Gil Gilman, George Hallett and a man named Deimer, whose first name I never learned. I got their names later. The dying man's name was C. J. Reif, assistant foreman on a ranch owned by a cousin of the Boyds.

Reif was now pretty plainly done, and I ordered Hallett to take off his boots. He came forward to the body and did so and handed them to me with the spurs on. He then at my command handed me Reif's hat and I put it on.

As I backed out of the clear, I called the men all the names I could think of, and still they never moved. I lost sight of them when I turned beyond the trees to get my bay, and rode back then to the clear and still they had not moved.

They were terrified. I think sometimes human power in anger grows so great under pressure that it can work this effect. My father had been of this mind. Besides, there was not a man there who did not feel a sense of guilt. However, it was explained to me also later that the men knew of my skill with the rifle and thought by disappearing I was trapping them into making some move and that I would then shoot them down from the screen of trees. Certainly I had intimidated them so they did not hardly know where to move or turn.

But besides my hate, which held them, I still think in practical terms of the mental force of the rifle, an accurate, long-range weapon, much more deadly in the hands of a good shot than any hand-gun ever made.

To get out of there I rode to a little, clear rise under some trees about a mile away, and tried to pull myself together, thinking what I ought to do.

LOHMAN MEETS A RELATIVE

Ed's bay got nervous as I headed back for town. In the heat of day I had neglected his water. There was a small, poor-looking farm with a drip-trough, but no horse-trough, so I took a rock and put it at the down end and let her fill so the bay could drink.

Made enough noise to bring out the hands or the family but no one showed. House and barn both looked empty and the house had the shades down.

Took time to put my boots on. They fit fine. The hat was clear too big, so I threw it away. While I was doing this a man on a horse came past hitting it up for Socorro fast. So I knew the word would go ahead of me. I did not mind now, as I was on the aggressive and would shoot first if I decided to, not wait to be shot at.

The spurs I took off from the boots. They were fancy, cheap, poor-made, with Mex-looking rowels. I started to knock off the points with a rock, then threw them away.

I went back to the Socorro saloon at a jog. People along the streets were few but they saw me coming and I saw them disappear. I could hear running and talking back of buildings but no shot was fired at me. It seemed strange to see the same saloon now after all that had befallen me.

I walked in. At the front end, as I came in the back, a big 12-man poker game stopped and I recollected it was Saturday.

The cards stopped slapping. Someone called for a beer in a low voice. Redhead bartender showed nervousness, then moved to get it. About eight or nine men along the bar seemed to freeze. I leaned my rifle up neat against the bar, then took her back, put her on cock, leaned her again. Never moved my new Colt from the belt.

Took a better look at the place. I saw what I had not seen before, though unimportant, a gold eagle hanging over the back bar.

I looked over the men. Some were standing staring at me, some looked hard at the big door, or at the floor or at their whiskey glasses. For at least a minute there was no move, except the bartender sliding the beer glass. He slid it a long ways. It came to a slow stop. He started to polish a whiskey glass then. The card dealer had not moved, holding a half deck.

The bartender eased up to me. I said to him: "I found the place as you directed but it was not like you said."

"No?" he said in a low voice. "Did the best I could for you."

I believed him. Said I wanted a glass of milk.

Said friendly: "We have quite a few calls for milk, plain or with brandy, which is a faddish drink right now, but just now am out of milk."

Said I would settle for a glass of water. He got it for me, refused my money, and I drank it slowly.

As I put down the glass, there was a small, quick move up front. I turned but did not reach and could see nothing. The sound resembled a match striking but I saw no lighted match.

I said: "If there are people who want business with me, they can have it. I have just now come from the cotton-wood grove north of town."

Nobody spoke. I said then: "I would like to ask if there are any Boyds here which I do not recognize. If so, I would like for them to come out with me."

Nobody spoke.

"Or relatives or dear friends."

Nobody spoke nor moved.

The bartender walked to me slow: "Mr. Lohman, I surely and sincerely think that the people you are interested in are not here."

I had never been called mister before, it surprised me.

The bartender now brought out a Colt from under the bar. He laid it near my rifle and said: "If you intend to start shooting, Mr. Lohman, I will shoot, too, and right at you. I will not have my place shot up. It has been shot up once before and that I will not tolerate. I try to run a clean place."

I told him I had no intention of trying to shoot up the place. I told him I never shot without having a sharp-showed target and would not start now. I told him if any shooting was to be done, it would not be within doors except to protect myself.

"In that case," the bartender said, "it is different."

He removed his gun from the bar. He now had the advantage of me. All the advantage, and he knew it. It is peculiar how this thing works. It is hard to explain how a peaceable man can get an advantage, no matter whether the man he faces is inclined to murder him or is a fair-play man. The man with the nerve has the real throwdown.

My father had explained this to me many times, saying that in his lifework, for every man he had arrested while being armed, he had arrested one while being unarmed. My father felt that both his sons would have been alive if they had gone to arrest their men without being armed.

I said goodbye, picked up my belongings and went out.

I had not forgotten Ed Hoffman nor that Jake might still be at Reamer's Livery Barn, so I rode there. George Reamer was there and so was Blacky and I told Reamer what I had come for.

He asked me to wait and that he would call Ed, who to my surprise was sleeping in his hay loft. He got Ed down. Ed had been drinking heavy the night before and at first I thought his attitude to me had something to do with my trouble. But later I found out he knew nothing about it.

He looked over his horse, said he was satisfied. I thanked him and he just nodded. Then he went into Reamer's office and stretched out on a pile of newspapers and went to sleep again.

Reamer, who was a man about 60 with a bald head, listened to what I had to say and said I owed him a dollar for Blacky's keep. I unsewed a dollar from my pants and gave it to him. He said he knew he could not get it out of Ed, who had a hangover and was without funds, so I gave a couple more dollars to Reamer. Asked him to give them to Ed.

He had some trouble finding the blanket and strap I rode Blacky with, as of course Ed had rode him with the same equipment I had. I realized then that when I took the bay I had not been in a saddle on a horse since the Boyds shot Jimmy.

While he was seeking for the blanket, I asked him if he had seen Jake Leffertfinger. He said yes he had gone to Magdalena two days before with another man of the same name as mine.

I was knocked silly, though having heard of Harley before from the bartender. I asked if the first name was Harley. Reamer said he did not know. We had no sooner finished this conversation than a man rode into the stable and I saw it was my brother Harley.

Seeing the rider and not knowing him at first, I had slid into a box stall but now came out.

I said: "Hello, Harley."

Harley stared. Finally he said: "Hello, Tot." We shook hands.

Harley said, "Just a minute," and went to talk to Reamer. They talked in low tones. Then Harley came back. He motioned me into the box stall where I had first hidden from him.

Harley said: "I have been to the saloon where you held them up. The man you attacked upriver is dying. The way you did him scares folks. Why did you do it, Tot?"

I asked him if he really did not know. He said that he had only recently ridden back into town after going only part way to Magdalena with Jake.

"Harley," I said, "our father is dead." Then I told him.

Harley sat down on a loose feedbox in the stall. Finally he said: "I will have to take some time to think this over."

I said: "You stay here and take some time to think it over and I will do something about it." I then told him about Shorty Boyd, my time with Restow, about spooking the Boyds' herd and shooting Nelson and the rest. At first I could not believe my father had omitted telling him about Shorty Boyd but later realized it was a little like my father to keep his mouth shut even with his own kin.

Harley said: "I should of stayed at home, why did I leave?"

I said: "Yes, Harley, you should of stayed to help me with Father."

"I'll ride up to Oklahoma with you."

I said: "That's not far enough. I am riding to Wyoming, maybe further, but first to Bradley's place at Santa Rosa." I was noticing how well dressed Harley was.

"Hunter Boyd is in Santa Rosa," Harley said. "I heard it on the street last week and heard it again here this morning. Some kind of a cattle deal."

I said I would go there looking for Hunter Boyd.

Harley seemed to get a little excited. I closed my eyes, while he ran a good deal at the mouth. The way he talked brought him back to me as a kid. With eyes closed I was seeing him as a kid.

When we were young, all kids together, Harley would sometimes show slowness, which my brothers thought was weakness. Like the time of the Comanche raid on our place. We wanted him to help us get the horses into the barn, and he showed slowness until my brother Nevin called him on it. At these times it was as if Harley was fighting some weakness. That's how it seemed now. He kept talking, but kept his eyes on a corner of the box stall where I had hid from him.

"You meet me in four days at the Muleshoe—" he said this several times—"that is a place in Santa Rosa. We will hole up together. There are places up there where the two of us holed up could stand off an army. I'm with you in this. I owe you something for leaving the family like I did."

I said I would see him at the place.

He kept coming back to the idea. "The reason I want to stay around is to investigate this terrible thing that's been done to our father, and to see what the community thinks of you."

I told him I could tell him that.

"But I've got to go to the bottom of this."

I said: "Yes, Harley."

"I'm with you, I'm with you," he kept saying. He went to his horse and pulled out a pretty fair Winchester. He began slinging it around, snapping open the breech and so on. "I haven't used this gun since they deputized me at Los Piños."

I said, "Oh Harley, have you been to Los Piños?"

"You bet," said Harley, "I was there."

He put the gun back and led the animal around and mounted. "Well—at Santa Rosa at the Muleshoe."

Though I knew my brother was a liar, it was a cure for loneliness to see him.

Harley waved as he rode off.

Within fifteen seconds I was on Blacky and getting out of town fast toward the south pass over the big ridge. But as I rode along I was worried and thought till my brains ached. When I had come to Socorro I was weak and did not eat much of the bartender's food. But on getting to the grove, from there on could not recall being weak. And then had decided I would rampage and kill off quite a few. But even while talking to Harley had even felt this idea shrinking up inside of me. Decided then and there this strong feeling cannot stay long with a man. All that was left of my feeling at the grove was that at least I would call out Hunter Boyd at Santa Rosa or shoot him on sight.

Wondered how I looked to people. Both on the way to Reamer's Livery Barn and later getting out of town after seeing Harley I had noticed people shrunk away from me in doorways and such, though Reamer had not seemed scared. Decided some had heard like the men at the saloon and some had not.

-18-

LOHMAN GOES TO A PARTY

It was near night when I got into Santa Rosa, a pretty town. I was still on the watch for the Boyds, but had seen nothing of them. Saw nothing in town to lead me to believe they were there. Stopped in a saloon to ask the way to the Bradleys and was directed well. There was a big moon and clouds that looked as if nature might be shaping for a cold spell, but the night was pleasant.

Seven miles north of town I saw the Bradley place and was knocked flat by it, it was so big. It was a typical Mex house with low construction and extending everywhere. From it came the strong smell of flowers. There was a patio with some nice-looking trees, and a lot of the grounds were walled in all the way to the barns.

I wanted to just stop, deliver the notes Amos had asked me to. I was still thinking of either the Oklahoma or Wyoming proposition. I felt shy about hitching and going to the door. But as I got near the house I could tell something was going on, for music was being played. You could hear a good deal of talk inside the house and on the patio.

The house door was closed. A lot of light was coming from the windows around it, but I banged the door, at first easy, then hard. The door flew open and I was knocked flat by seeing Amos Bradley.

He stared at me, and then yelled and laughed, and then said: "Get in here fast as you can."

I walked in. He closed the door. There were some people coming across a big low room around the corner from where I stood, and I could not see them, but hear their voices coming closer.

Amos started across the room in usual fast style, me behind him. I would of been embarrassed just to be there, with the girls I saw and everybody else dressed fit to kill, all feeling good from what they had drunk. But now it was worse, with me in my stole boots but elsewhere rags that many a man would of been thrown out of a saloon for. Well, I was scared as a rabbit but followed close behind Amos, to not be seen, but he walked too fast. All at once here I was in the middle of the room. Amos was far ahead, so I found no cover.

Then he turned, seeing this good-looking woman who was in charge standing near where they had food and drink on the table. She was a beautiful, middle-age Spanish woman dressed up to make a fit partner for a rich vaquero. I saw her eyes meet Amos's eyes, as if saying who is this you are bringing here, so Amos suddenly wheeled and led me sort of into the hall, I walking like a led horse. This was the hall we had come from. We went up some small steps there, which puzzled me for the house had a big set of steps inside the big room. Now these little, narrow steps were like opening up a cupboard door and going up steps inside.

Up there was an office Amos had fixed for himself and a little bedroom.

He got me up there then in the other room, lighted a lamp and closed the door. All this time whenever I started to say something, he made signs to keep mum. But he kept smiling, so I knew he was not exactly angry about seeing me.

There was a little bed in the room. There was nice furniture and the whole house seemed to smell of flowers. I could also smell food cooking, and now the music I could hear plain from down in the patio.

I got in a word then. I said: "I thought you were in Oklahoma."

Amos said: "I thought you were dead."

I told him not yet.

"Well, we couldn't get through," Amos said. "We couldn't get through, so we came back. Everybody up around Clayton told us not to try it. Those Utes are making some trouble. They say they have hooked up in places with the Comanches. That is possible. But anyhow we could not get through and so are back here. This is a good thing. You are just in time for the party tonight. One of my daughters, my own kid, is getting herself engaged, and this is a sort of half-American half-Mex shindig we are putting on here. You will fit in fine. There is so many damn squaws here that you will practically be snowed under, which will be good for you. Also your friend, Nita, is here naturally and will be glad to see you."

I told Amos I could not think of staying. How the Boyds were hot on my trail. I filled in as much as seemed wise about what had happened since he saw me, just to warn him and make him understand my presence in the house was dangerous and would continue to be.

But he just sat there and laughed at me. "You mean to say Hunter Boyd or any of his bums would come here? Listen, Hunter Boyd is in Santa Rosa."

I told him I had heard that in Socorro.

He waved his hand with a sneer about Boyd and kept talking about him. "Listen, this house is well taken care of, so don't you fret about Hunter Boyd and his bums and his crazy sons. I cannot handle Boyd maybe in the clear or even in this man's town on the broad street, but here I can handle him. This place is well taken care of. Know what you are going to do? You are going to this party, whether you like it or not. You stay here tonight. This is the safest place in Santa Rosa for you. Where's your father?"

I had not told him this, but now I told him, even though it went against my father's dignity.

"Oh no," he said. "Oh no." Then he got up from the bed and began talking to himself low, as he had up north. Then he began to curse and rave. Then he mumbled again, standing at the window looking out, which was strange as the music was playing down there in the patio, typical Mex music, with Amos mumbling all through it. Then he sat on the bed. I had not tried to stop any of this, as he was my host of course. Also because I saw it was relieving his mind.

Pretty soon he said, "Wait here." The minute he was out of the room, I scanned from the windows and got the lay of the place in case of a quick slope down by a rope or by vines to get out of there. Whiles I was doing this Amos came back with a colored man.

Amos saw what was in my mind and said, "Oh no, you don't, Tot. No getting out of this. Now here you are and here I am and here is where you will stay until I talk to Boyd tomorrow. This time I will have some heavy stuff to use on Boyd."

They got a pair of Amos's pants which I cuffed up from the bottom as he was a shade taller than me. Otherwise they fit fine. And Amos made me put on one of his silk shirts.

But first they brought up a tub with pails and the colored man helped me take a bath with hot water, which I surely needed, not having had a hot tub bath for a long time. Amos stood there and laughed at me, seeing how I enjoyed it. The man also cut my hair.

And while all this was going on Amos kept talking with hardly a stop, explaining the household, saying that back some years he had been a ranch manager for this rich widow of a Mexican. How she had already three daughters, and he had finally married her and they had three more. But Nita was not any of these. She was an adopted daughter. She had been close to one of the girls. When orphaned the Bradleys had taken her in, like one of their own children.

Downstairs and Amos had arranged it for a surprise. So that when the girls of the house knew who I was, having been told about me by Nita, they came around me like a swarm.

The names of the three Mexican daughters of the house were Rosita, Mary and Conchita, and the oldest, Mary, and Conchita were married and had husbands and children. Then Amos's children by his Mexican wife had the names Helen, Frances and Sophronia. The party was for Helen's troth.

Well, it was some strange the way they acted. They said quite a good deal in Spanish, some of which was quite simple to understand. They kept coming up and looking at me very curious.

Then they would all stand back in a row, looking at me, waving their fans.

They laughed a good deal among themselves, using many Spanish words to hook up with "caballero."

They were soft in everything they did. They seemed kinder, except for my mother, than most women I had seen. They seemed to be more fluttery.

Well, the children were there, too, dressed up to kill like Mex women dress their children for best. Amos's wife came in, who I had seen before. She was sure a beauty. I was surprised, she having had so many children. She looked no more than forty. She was a real Mex beauty, with a satin dress and a mantilla and headdress. I had never seen such black eyes in a woman. You could only guess her age when near enough to see the eye wrinkles. Of course she was pretty heavy painted. The girls did not wear much of this.

On a big table in one corner was the greatest variety of food ever—both Mexican and American. The tortillas were of fine flour and you could of floated them on the Grande. Then they had sugar tits and desserts.

Around the food table must have been about fifty and about fifty more dancing at this end of the patio where this orchestra was playing.

But then all of a sudden they began to fire off firecrackers outside. They had planned for some better fireworks later in the distance just beyond the edge of the grounds. It was a wonderful party.

When the firecrackers started, the crowd began to move outside and two of the girls, Rosita and Helen, stayed near me and I turned around in the silence and there was Nita.

I found out afterwards when she found I was there she went up and changed her dress again. I don't know what she wore before. It made her blend in with the place, for there were flowers all over—this red flower hibiscus, some artificial, some real, and lilies—the Mex people are great for lilies. She seemed to come out of flowers.

Well, she just stood there, and we did not say a thing. We went out to the patio way at the far end away from the dancing. She showed me a little stone bench behind some lemon trees up against the wall, and we sat down there and with the shade of the trees between us and the house, the music seemed far away. We just kept sitting there. Finally I asked her how she was and she said fine. She asked me how I was and I said I was all right.

After the fireworks had finished, we moved further out in the patio. It may be I should have said something, knowing I was moving out soon, but have never been much of a talker, and of course I felt in a certain way about this girl. I could see she was nervous and maybe even angry at me for being so quiet.

Did not know how to handle this situation, so happened to think years back to Nevin, who could not seem to write a letter to a friend who had invited him to a party which he could not attend, because he was going to Fort Worth. He asked my mother what he should say. My mother said: "Well, Nevin, that's what you should write your friend, merely tell him why and he will understand." So Nevin wrote: "Dear Friend Joe, will be unable to attend your party being in Fort Worth on said date, Nevin Lohman." Nevin would not change it for Mother and me, so all I did was fix the misspelled words.

So now this came to me and I decided to tell this girl why. I explained that not having anything to say was not because I did not care to talk to her, but that I had not had much practice. Had never been to a party like this at any time in my life, except just little bees at schoolhouses and once in a while go to sit and watch the older people dance.

She kept nodding her head and turning it away from me and then turning back, so that I thought maybe she was turning from me in disgust. But then I saw that this was not so.

I told her that I had never felt the lack of parties, not being used to them, and that I was a sort of outdoors person, been so all my life. Well, this was an interesting thing to talk about, I mean how people are different, so we talked about that awhile and here I found I was talking good, going from subject to subject with her. We discussed the various features of the earth and nature, and horses in which I found she was interested.

She saw after a while I was getting nervous and I admitted to her I wanted to know what was going on outside the house. I put this in a way not to scare her too much. Then all at once she said she had an idea about giving me a view of the outside. So we moved away from the party then, up the small stairs where Amos had first taken me, and on the landing just outside the door of the place he used for an office she showed me this small door in the wall. It was not secret, just part of the wall panel that swung out showing steps going up to a kind of tower.

She led the way up. In the part on the level with the hall, it was so dark I thought we ought to go back and get a light, but the stairs turned and from there on up after the first four or five steps of the turn, the moonlight showed the rest of the way from the broke-out windows at the top.

Well, she said when the house was built this was supposed to be a scanning place to sight Indians from. That tower must have taken a sight of rain in a fall, with the windows all broke out, but it was mostly stone constructed down to where the stairs began, so probably made no difference.

To the south I could see nothing, to the west nothing, but—whoap—over to the north there was a man and a mount standing motionless under a small tree, as if trying to keep in shadow. Then over eastward towards the Texas state line there were four others, with six mounts, standing near a small grove, so that they and the trees looked as if painted on the ground by the moonlight. Flat-like they were.

She noted all this with me, but neither of us said much. There was no doubt in my mind that the Boyds were watching the house, but what could I do? As we watched, the lone man got on his horse and rode south a piece and then got off again.

Well, here we are again, I said to myself. Can't even shake the Boyds at this party. But as I thought of Hunter Boyd, I decided it had come to this—that I would have to call out Hunter Boyd in the open, or one of his sons, and at least have a kill-shot in their direction.

When we came down then, the girls joined up with us. Nita and I had little to say from then on that night because we were amongst folks. Two of the girls and two young Mex boys did a Mex dance in the house, with the orchestra coming in from outside. Most of the orchestra was by this time pretty far gone. The slow music was quaverish in spots, but when they got into a fast dance this did not show. They played their heads off. The dance was wonderful. One boy had knuckle-bones and danced to them after without music, the girls making a line behind him and following him around waving colored kerchiefs.

Amos came up, he having had a good deal to drink. He had had trouble with Mrs. Bradley, I could see from a distance. He was drinking tequila like water. He practically forced some on me. This I sipped at. He slapped me on the back considerable and told me to loosen up. I told him I understood and was for a fact enjoying myself, but had to think of my hand.

"Also, the eye."

"Yes, the eye."

He had a drink in his left hand then and grabbed my hand with his right, holding it up, starting to make a speech about my hand, but Mrs. Bradley stopped him. She told him good. She saw I was embarrassed. She saw I did not want to drink. She said all this in Spanish, a lot of which I hitched onto, other words I lost. She next took my hand and led me over to the coffee. The coffee was wonderful compared to what I had packed and drunk back in Texas. It was sweetened to taste like sugar almost with a strong effect. I told her I could get drunk on this coffee, that this coffee was enough. She said it was the best way.

Nita had been standing with the other girls, all ordered to bed so the old folks could get the music people out of the house, also others who did not seem to wish to get home.

Mrs. Bradley was shooing the girls up and out, I knowing how strict they are, people like Mrs. Bradley. But Nita did not seem to mind, pressing my hand hard, and saying she would see me in the morning.

In bed I tried to sleep but first had no luck, but finally dozed off. When I woke up it was still dark but showing light in the east. Not likely to sleep again, so got up lit the candle and nosed around.

In the little office beside my room I could see pencils and paper, Amos's, stashed. They were better stuff than I had ever seen before, especially the pencils. I could sure write well with them, so sat down and started a letter to Restow and it got longer and longer filled with my wanderings. I got out the stowed stuff I had kept from away back, though some of this I had left with Restow.

But I had many sheets of neat-ruled paper from the place up near Clayton where I had met the Bradleys and later at the Bawbeens where Mrs. Bawbeen gave me two more sheets of it. This was all pretty full, so I went on from there. The more I put down the better I liked doing it as when I started the harness list for my father back there.

I got it all up to the place where I met Jake and later the Hoffmans, but tried to write about how I had gone to the grove. Could not do this at this time, so decided to write later, leaving a gap and telling about Harley and the redhead bartender. Praised my people a good bit, they deserved it. I would of liked more people to know about my father, and how he was for a fact.

For a time I watched the sun getting higher, then would think of something to fill in, so would go back and put it there. Sun got higher. Sat, watching it, regretting somewhat I had not sloped off the night before. Went up the steps to the scanning place and was plain mortified. Stumped plain.

Some of the people I had feared the night before were people of the Bradleys! Found this out when I saw coffee brought from the Bradley kitchen by the cook to them. These were near riders, scattered around, four I counted.

But then I saw others more distant, some I had seen the night before, they were getting no coffee and were Boyds all right.

I got tired watching, went downstairs and here was the folks getting ready to sit down. There was fine food on the breakfast-spread. I still was hungry from away back and Amos said they would fatten me up. They had hot cakes like North Texas, and mountain fish, small but good. They had a platter of pig meat, mostly fat, which only Amos ate of. He said he needed this for the results of the night before and sure looked it.

Along toward noon Mrs. Bradley had to take one of the girls to the doctor, so all the girls went along, even Nita. Nita wanted to stay, but Mrs. Bradley said no, looking at me, smiling.

I showed Amos what I had been doing with the pencils and he said: "That's right. Put it down about your father, though. Put it down."

Well, so it went and about midafternoon the girls came back with Mrs. Bradley, and I came down from upstairs where I had worked and Nita and I went out on the patio. Sat there till suppertime. Amos surprised me, not so much the others, by saying he would have the musicians back again that night. But he had an argument with Mrs. Bradley about this. He said: "Why hell, a wedding lasts a week, an engagement party should run up at least to two days." He may have had other reasons, possibly to show the Boyds, and to get our spirits up again. Also as an excuse to get drunk. Mostly the latter I think.

Well, it was as would of been expected. The people who came were tired out from the night before. They stood around polite and stiff-like. They evidently liked Amos and came to please him. They had a few drinks and sat around, talking in low voices. Some of the girls danced with each other, for men were few. The five men of the orchestra were only partly there. Two of them were in the calabozo for drunk and fighting. The music was all right but sort of quiet and mournful, except for one or two times when they played for fast dancing. They played The Dove beautiful, which is a beautiful piece.

Amos was going good and drank a lot, going from person to person.

I spoke to Nita two or three times and finally we sat down, and was surprised at the ideas she had for us to do. She evidently had been thinking a lot, which made it troublesome for me. She said one thing: "I kissed you up north but here we have not kissed." I said I would when not so many people were around.

I said: "I am getting off soon for Wyoming."

"Alone?" she said.

"Well, had planned it that way."

"How about together?" This surprised me.

"It's a hard life."

"Might be harder to stay here."

"You mean us."

"I mean me."

"Oh."

Then I said: "Here you are surrounded by friends and comfort which you would tend to miss."

"There are other things to be considered."

"Well, I suppose so."

She said nothing, and I said: "Let us talk it over in the morning."

She said, and I could see she was vexed: "You are in no position to come and go here because the house is being watched. You'd better consult someone."

"Amos?"

"Or me."

I agreed to that, but said I could not stay forever.

"A comfortable long time is not forever."

Well, this got me to pondering.

I said to myself now here is a young girl not responsible for her acts. I will have to act according. This young girl, I said, should not become involved with me at this time. But I felt a yearning towards her, and several times in talking to her began to say to myself: "Now here I am telling her about my various problems of life, except the big one, just as natural." But I watched my talk careful. But at the same time feeling this yearning power.

Once when I was listening a good deal and later sitting and merely enjoying the quiet with her, I saw tears in her eyes. Now if I had been a ninny I would of thought she was sorry for me. But knew she was a high-strung girl, and only vexed with me for not talking more.

She had done a lot for me along with Amos and had given me this pin like an H later a T which I had. I had given her nothing. So in the afternoon I thought about this and took the only Mex dollar I had among the remaining others sewed in my jeans, and marked the soft Mex dollar with an N and a T. I ground these letters down with my knife. Then I thought of making it to a ring, but had no savvy, so went to the sheds and made a ring of a horseshoe nail like kids wear. I gave her the dollar and the ring, and the way she acted you would have supposed I had given her a horse. She bust out crying by this act of mine. I regretted it some. It gnawed completely at my mind.

Soon she said she was tired and would go to bed, and hoped I would be careful. I told her I would be, and was careful in discussing this, not wishing to fret her, not knowing how much

Amos had bore down with her. I told her I had slept well the night before, and would get more rest that night.

We walked to the patio. We shook hands while the other people were leaving and not watching. After a while it was natural, Amos being out back somewhere, for me to go up where Nita and I had been the night before, to ponder about having been there with her and for a good look around.

That little high old place was as before. The night was pretty dark. Nothing much to be seen, as the clouds were heavy and moon not up yet. But whiles I was there three men on horses rode up to the gate, two stayed mounted and one got off and walked in. Too dark to see who they might be.

But after some time when I came to the stair turn, standing in the dark, I could see the hall bare, so stayed in the dark and froze when I heard the voices. Through the small stair door and the door to Amos's office which was wide open, I could see Amos talking to Hunter Boyd.

The first I thought was to call out Boyd, except that no one but a fool calls a man out in the dark of a night. But I decided different then, because the conversation interested me.

Amos was saying: "I have a book here."

He went out of my sight probably to a shelf and came back with a very old book, with most of the pages falling out. He pulled up a bench close to Boyd.

Hunter Boyd was saying: "It's not a case of power. It's a case of law and order. We cattlemen are determined to bring law and order into this country."

"That kind of law sounds lawless."

"You are playing on words, Amos. We still have the Constitution of the United States to fall back on. I think that's still in force. They don't think much about it in Texas, but I guess we do here."

Amos rubbed his chin and looked at Boyd. "Constitution?" He laughed.

"Well, it's the basic law of the land."

Amos showed the book. He seemed excited. "Hunter, I'm glad you mentioned it. Quite a coincidence, though they's been a lot of tall talk floating around. Not all coincidence. I'm glad to know you think it means something."

"I certainly do," said Boyd.

"Hunter, you and your friends don't know shucks about the Constitution." Amos stopped fluffing the book pages: "All right, here's what the Constitution states: It says here that a man for a crime cannot be put twice in jeopardy of his life. Know what jeopardy means? Danger. You cannot put a man where you are endangering or threatening his life two times for one offense against the law. That's law and order according to the Constitution. Well, with your brand of law and order you have hounded this boy from Texas to Socorro in the territory. You have shot his horse and made him walk miles for water. You sent other men against him who tried repeatedly to kill him and failed. You have made him fear for his life every night he laid his head on the ground. You have done all this because he killed your son in self-defense. You have done and are still doing this to a poor orphan of eighteen years of age. Placed his life in danger twice? You have done it about sixteen dozen times. And by God, you are hounding him still and will hound him to his grave. So don't, Hunter, ever talk to me again about law and order and that damn hypocrisy."

Hunter Boyd got up and merely looked at Amos. I could hear Hunter Boyd's breath plain.

Amos had worked himself up and now he was really mad.

Hunter Boyd moved to the door, and stood there with his slitty eyes and white hair, and the bad hand sticking up like a claw.

Amos threw the book with all his force at Hunter Boyd's feet. The book landed solid and its pages flew all over. A couple of them went in the updraft almost up to Boyd's middle, so that he put out his hand to push them off, as if he was afraid they'd land in his face.

"There," said Amos, "that's what you and your friends are doing to the Constitution."

Hunter Boyd stood there looking at Amos for a minute. Then he said with his face white and his voice trembling: "I will call my men off the house." He spaced out the words, being hardly able to talk. "But tomorrow from daylight, he has two hours to leave town. Two hours. Then the relief is off."

"I may keep him here indefinitely."

"At your own risk."

"What do you mean by that?"

"I would not come here. Some of the others might."

"They better not."

Hunter Boyd reached for the open door handle with his claw hand, the cigar in the other. I saw the cigar tremble and spill ash. I heard him going down the stairs very slowly, picking each step with care. Then I heard the front door close. The mournful music was playing again, and it sounded a little as if the musicians had had a lot to drink by this time, but the violin was still good.

Well, here I am alone doing the last writing I'll probably do in the Bradley place. That conversation I heard between Amos and

Old Man Boyd shows me what is bound to occur if I stay here. I just went downstairs to go through the place and make sure I can get out without disturbing anyone or getting myself in a bind. Everybody has gone to sleep and I have an idea Amos is deeper down than anyone else because he sure had a lot to drink before he went to bed.

Everything I could think of I took in view. When the time comes all I have to do is walk down through the main section of the house, then through the pantry and kitchen, then through a covered piece to the shed where they keep the wagons and then through this to the shed where Blacky is. I have already spotted him in the same box stall he was in when I was out there this afternoon making the ring for Nita. In the kitchen I will have to be carefullest because the help is laid out there like timber, with the Mex cook sleeping right in the middle of the floor with a serape over his head, but completely drunk all right.

I have done pretty well with the letters to Restow which Amos will see are properly handled. Sure have produced a lot of hen-tracked paper. People will see from them that there were two sides to this question and certainly if they read carefully will see the kind of a man my father was. I suppose that is the main reason I wrote more down about this trip than I ever did before, except, of course, I found out it is a relief to a some-troubled mind. I have heard this before, my mother saying when rough times came she usually sat down and wrote to her sister and her sister the same. . . .

Have just scanned around from the place above and appears that the Bradley people either got tired and went home or were worked on by the Boyds and sickened of the trouble and left, except there is one man on the front gate, and one more fooling around the shed back of the patio away from the other sheds. I looked into this one yesterday and Amos has a rig and a couple of broke-down dish-wheel wagons stored there.

No Boyds or their people in sight, but they may have pulled back to bait me into the clear. Will go in the early gray when people get tired and careless of watching, and when I have a fair chance of seeing my way in strange country, though I would scarcely call this night dark. There is a small creek, plumb-dry but deep cut and possible for cover about 90 feet behind the horse sheds and may use this. . . .

Have just written a note to Amos. Getting on towards light. Have been looking at an open box of Amos's shell which would fit my chamber, lying along with full boxes. But have pondered this and will leave with only my own 16 shell, as there are two chances open and will have to meet one or the other.

-19-

THE LETTERS OF BRADLEY
AND RESTOW

Letter from Restow to Amos Bradley

(Letter was never delivered and ultimately returned to Restow.)

Dear *Mr. Bradley: Your letter reached me after quite a space, though the new train service I can't complain of. In just the last few days I have heard some disturbing news about Lohman, and in the light of the kind interest you took in your letter I thought I might inquire if you have seen or heard of him. Not only was the news getting bad about Lohman but there is a rumor around here about even worse concerning his father. Believe me, I would come down there and see what I can do to help the boy but the situation up here makes it downright impossible for me to move at this time and, since I must be getting chicken-hearted in my old age, I seem to grow more and more disturbed about Comanche trouble*

*to the west of us which makes the west and south leg of a travel
triangle out of the question just now. Besides, I'm wondering when
the braves will pay me a call here as they have been sighted near
the state line several times heading this way. Let me know what
you hear.*

Faithfully yours,
Restow

Letter from Restow to Amos Bradley

(This letter was delivered, having been written after the above
letter failed to reach him. It was written and received within two
weeks of mailing by Restow, but the writing and receipt took
place nearly one year after the events of the party at Bradley's
home and the departure of Lohman from the Bradley hacienda
early the next morning. Bradley's reply follows the letter.)

*Dear Amos: My letter written almost a year ago never reached
you, so I'm trying again with a fresh start. Having heard nothing
of T. J. Lohman for almost a year and a half but having definitely
ascertained that Lohman's father was executed by misguided per-
sons, I am anxious to know what became of his son. Up here the
word is that he is somewhere in Wyoming, which seems likely as
he was talking about that part of the country incessantly when he
worked for me. I expect to make the first trip into the territory I
have made in five years the middle of next month and will be in
Santa Rosa and neighboring regions for quite a spell. Let me know
if you will be available for a visit when I get down there, as am
most anxious to bridge the gap of months and news. My respects to
you and your family.*

Restow.

Dear Restow: Glad to get your letter, saying you will be down this way. The new mail service is O.K., isn't it? Well, I could tell you quite a tale in writing about the Lohman boy, but suffice to say for the present that I know he is not in Wyoming. I fervently wish he was. But instead of making a lot of hen tracks on paper, and inasmuch as you expect to amble down here soon, will wait to tell you all about it from my own lips. . . .

Well, am looking forward to your visit. I had expected to be in Mexico about the end of July, but that has been put off temporarily. Will await your visit. Will make sure I am here to see you. Come right to my place and don't fool with the hotels, there are two, both poorly.

Amos Bradley

STATEMENT BY AMOS BRADLEY TO RESTOW ON THE OCCASION OF HIS VISIT

(The events here recounted by Amos Bradley are those that followed the party at the Bradley hacienda at which Lohman was a guest and when Lohman early the next morning took French leave of the Bradley family.)

W *ell, this is my story about the Kid, one that sank deep in my mind, and have told by request so many times that at last one of my daughters put it down in writing, and she was the same one who helped to neaten up the Kid's stuff.*

I was dizzy as a wasp when I got up. The thing was on my conscience and so I ambled for the Kid's bed and of course he was not there. Might have known but what was I to do. Also found a note from Lohman, and read it and stowed it away, noting at the same time that my shell, which we had discussed the night before

and which fit his rifle as well as mine, was not disturbed. Also there
was a sizable half-sealed envelope that told me on the outside what
it contained, so did not bother it for the time being. But altogether
things did not seem to cinch up.

Gave some thought about what to do. With a parcel of women
about to bust itself around my head I was in bad shape. First it
would be Nita when she knew the boy was gone. Then the whole
shackful of Spanish-hearted females would probably drive me crazy
after he had made such a ten-strike with them the night before.

I wanted none of that, so I went out to the kitchen and kicked
up José who was lying in the middle of the floor with a blanket over
him from mucha tequila. Told him a whole gallon of coffee and
that greaser never ground the beans and boiled the water so fast.
I got a saddle on Jake and led him around to the kitchen. I doused
my head in the horse trough a couple of times, got down five cups
strong enough to float a gold nugget and then made José fix the rest
in a quart mescal bottle with a rope net. Got on my horse and got
out of there.

It seemed sense that the Lohman boy would go north for a hole-
up. Something I had noticed about Lohman besides other good
traits was his judgment of country, which is light handy to have in
this part of it, seeing that a seasoned line rider or such can get himself into plenty of trouble quarter mile from his base camp without
trying too hard. I figured if the Kid took the bridge road north
he would ride smack into a hole-up he could not miss, a funnel-
shaped canyon as long as from here to Cuba, with a steep rise that
had good rock cover. The place had various and sundry names like
Sawhorse Canyon and the Big Slide. Other less imaginative people
called it just a hell of a place to be. The Indians from way back
called it Hole in the Sky. Yet I could not be sure, the Kid might have

spurned it and rode on north and made a clean break for Wyoming as he had hinted to me the night before. But what he did not know and I was pretty sure about was that the Boyds people were watching all roads out of Santa Rosa and probably the north road special with maybe even a few rolled rocks to slow up a fast rider.

About a mile from home heard horsefeet and turned and saw Nita riding on that little mare of hers. I stopped and abused the girl. Abused is the word. I am ashamed of what I said to her, but the objective was reached and she turned back. But if looks could have killed . . .

I went on. The sky was getting bright and the sun was rimming up real good, and it looked like a nice day. I pushed Jake the first miles and then heard a shot ahead and then some more. Next I saw sitting on his horse George Beaton, with whom I had never been good friends since he grew 400 cows taller, with consequent damage to his formerly sweet personality. So I was not in the mood to more than howdy him and not too warm at that. He started to say something possibly about my sour looks but I staved him off. I knew what he was there for—to watch the back trail in case Lohman foxed to the rear. Ahead of me was the big prone finger of gradual rise, masking the steep slope beyond and this, of course, I could not see yet. This rise jutted out enough to make my forward trail curl like a snake, first sharp right around the base and sharp left across the flat beyond. I knew when I rode around that dirt finger I would probably see what I came for. And did.

There spread across the big down end of the funnel was quite a party. The other end of the funnel reached the sky and the target seemed to be up there, but right before me lower down was what looked like two dozen mule and wagon trains scattered by Sioux. All the elite had come out for the show. There was horses and men on them, and spring wagons and buckboards. Over to the left was the brave cattlemen surrounding Hunter Boyd. They were looking very serious-like and scanning the rise with fancy glasses now and then. In the middle was us common people, and to the right was the saloon gentry of Santa Rosa. Most of these people was trying appear that they had not carefully posted themselves out of rifle range and trying to act nonchalant, with their hands in their pockets, or on hips, chewing tobacco and spitting careful.

Situation was easy to read at first glance. Up toward the top with blue sky behind, was a boulder, big as a church, behind which Lohman was making his stand. Might have been a mile up the rise. Sprinkled like sheep-marbles down the slope was about four or five men including young Tom Boyd (I found this out later) and they were whaling away at the boulder in a kind of stupid way at the rate of about a shot a minute. Tom was using a big rifle that carried a heavier weight of grain than I knew existed and made a lot of noise against the clean, thin plunk of the other guns and now and then a shotgun blast like dry sticks rattling.

Apparently no shooting from the other end—Tot was saving his shell, as always. It seemed likely to me that the boy was depending on his own supply, having left my cache at the house untook from. Some people are too damned independent.

I cut my sights over to the left where Hunter and his people were directing the operations. "Well, gentlemen," I says. "The fox is up the rise but where are your fine, red coats." Hunter's face at this point would have colored a coat all right.

Nothing else happened, so I sat my horse and listened to the boys up the hill bang away. It went on for quite some time, with every once in a while the shots getting thicker when some attacking gent decided it was well to show enthusiasm.

I turned my attention for a while to the Santa Rosa crowd, which included some of the most outstanding drink cadgers in the region, congratulated them on their feeling for law and order and suggested that somebody ought to hire a hall and make a speech or if the show kept up for a reasonable time it might be good to mule-tow a bar out here and serve drinks.

I saw Ferdy Maxwell edging to me across from the cattle crowd, looking apologetic. He pointed out to me the three men Tot had hit so far. Two had their right arms shawled up around the shoulder with bloody rags. Naturally they had been on the left-hand side of the slope. But the cowpoker who was on the ground with gray death in his face had picked the bad side—the right, and he had got it slantwise and long and mean in the left leg, seeing how a man getting off shots from a reclining position up a high rise will throw out his left leg natural to brace a bead on the target.

Ferdy said in his soft-voiced apologetic way that so far the Kid had done good. He said as far as they could figure he'd gotten off only five shots and badly damaged three men. He explained then that Hunter Boyd had everything well organized and even had a man keeping a shot tally on the Kid, as they were pretty sure he was due to be starved out on cartridges.

I complimented Ferdy on Hunter Boyd's efficiency, and just at that minute the Kid got off a shot. It apparently came close to a shotgun toter with a sawed-off leg who was halfway up the slope, about even with Tom Boyd on the other side of the gut. I think the Kid maybe had drew blood as from where I sat my horse I could see Pegleg sucking at the back of his left hand. The shot was talked about considerable. I say this just to show you how simple-minded even growed men can get under stress of novel excitement.

Economy was the Lohman motto, but not on the other side. As soon as the slug from yonder was duly tallied, commented on and discussed freely on the basis of "How many's he got left?" the shooting enthusiasm on the downside hit a high mark. The boys blazed away at the rock, and twice in fifteen minutes a runty hunchback who portered a saloon owned by kin of the Boyds rolled himself up the slope like a crippled hoop with shell for the besiegers and a rifle for Peg-leg. He had a certain extent of guts, of course, moving in the open, but it was planned like that, it being as you know wrong to shoot a hunchback and considered beyond that the worse luck that can befall a man.

Bang, bang, bang, it went on like that, with not a shot from Lohman. The besiegers, of course, were covering the fact that they were not moving up the rise and were scared juiceless, doing their best with noise to show they were conscientious men.

About this time Boyd parted from the group and rode across my sights. I called to him, "Hunter, what are you trying to do, rock-drill him out from behind that dornick?"

Hunter tried to make out he didn't hear me and kept going over to the Santa Rosa people to say something.

Trying to figure a way to help Lohman, I tried to figure what I would do in Boyd's place. No chance of burning the Kid out, as there wasn't enough brush on that rise to warm the south end of a northbound louse. I thought of a powder charge then with a fuse, and hated myself for it instantly, thinking I might have loosed the idea in the air, because either by coincidence or something else I heard Hunter say "keg" to one of the Santa Rosa people, then turn and wave to Snake Biller, his new foreman, and Hal Carmody, his old, who was attending the shindig with his arm in a sling. Right away they wheeled their mounts and ran for town.

Hunter lingered with the Santa Rosa gentry.

Bang, bang, bang, it went on up the rise with no shots from Lohman. Bang, bang, bang. Only the emphasis was a little different because of Tom Boyd and his sheep gun. Every time that son of a bitch let go, it shook the ridge and I knew for a fact if it ever connected with Lohman it would blow him to China.

Now Hunter drifted back to his people across my front and I will say this, that I believe I killed Tom Boyd in the next five minutes just as if my hand had been aiming the rifle. I made a strong play to Hunter and this time he stopped without looking at me. As if he wanted and did not want to hear what I had to say.

Gabby as I was with a half a hangover and strong coffee and all, I said: "Why, for goodness sake, Hunter, if you want the Kid this bad, I may be able to talk him out of there, but what's the use of trying to ballast a mountain with lead. I've watched those boys up the rise now for half an hour and they merely bang off and don't move a hair toward the target. 'Fraid to. They are yellowed out and I cannot say I blame them, knowing how Lohman can shoot. Why not let me argufy with him, rather than more get hurt?" Course, I had to shout all this.

I could see Boyd wince, but the one who really did the wincing was Tom. It was plain, far as he was from where I sat my horse. He had heard every word in the lull and he could not stand that part about not moving. So now he moved possibly an inch, maybe a little more.

Upstairs there was another move behind the rock and a yellow dent in the blue. The shot's impact or the spasm of death, whichever it was, cartwheeled Tom Boyd ass over teakettle into the clear. It was like a man being drug by a lyncher or a doll pulled on a string. With his back bowed in a horrible way, he jerked and jerked on his head and heels in full view of all of us, then started rolling down the slide and never stopped till he rolled a quarter mile. The heavy gun came clattering down on top of him. He reached the flat and stopped with one leg clamped under his body looking like a rag doll a child had thrown away. And his post-mortem wind came out of his mouth in a big whish like "Uh" and then "Uh-h-h-h-" dying off. Old Man Boyd sat his horse and stared, never moved.

The shooting stopped. The four men left on the rise we had new respect for. No wonder they'd froze to base. They knew just how uncanny that little squirt was with his sawed-off Winchester. It would have been better for Tom if he had stayed yellow. He heard what I said and got a sudden rush of proud blood to the head and moved an inch. Dead.

After all the shooting it seemed very quiet. The men on the rise had craned their necks as much as they dared to see where Tom went, but, of course, their view was limited. But still they didn't shoot. Looked like men painted on the hillside. I half believe they were so concerned at the small move Tom had made which cost him his life that they were scared to move enough to pull a trigger. Or maybe they were just getting over the shock. I was, you might say, jolted out of my cogitations by somebody saying, "What's he throwing away—empty cartridges? What's he doing that for?" That turned my gaze up the rise and it was true, something was happening up by the big boulder, because I caught the glint of something bright in the air above the rock. Then there was more talk, then more quiet. It was like we knew in advance.

Ferdy had been kind enough to lend me his glasses now and then when I asked for them. Not that I needed them for ordinary purposes for the day was clear and the sun hot and bright, making everything on the slope sharp and clear. Toward the latter end of the shooting party, though, the sun began to dodge in and out among clouds and the light on the slope changed now and then, first shady, then streaked, then dark, and then bright again but when the big thing happened the sun was direct and clear and you could see details on the high rise like a gopher hole or a loose rock or pebble bigger than the rest. And you could see rock seams and small shadows made by deeper cuts.

Lohman came out from behind the boulder with his arms spread. He was the only one who was not surprised including me. I was speechless, so was Boyd, and there was a vague sound from some of the rest. As for the shooting men on the slope, they were so surprised that I am sure Lohman took about twenty steps and came out at least fifteen, twenty yards from cover before anyone exhibited presence of mind. Then all four let go and four slugs hit him in the chest, so that the shot pattern that I checked later was not more than two inches across. It lifted him off his feet and the sun did a curious thing. It seemed to hit him square and bright, as it had been hitting the boulder, so that his dark shirt for the minute seemed snow white and his chest seemed to cave. He fell down first on his knees, and then flat, with his hands now clasped, pushing the dirt and pebbles ahead of him like a plow as he slowly straightened out and was still.

After the noise there was dead quiet. The breeze had died. I looked once quick at the faces of the cattlemen and they were a study. Except Hunter who was smiling to himself so that, having known him thirty years, he visibly began to get small in my eyes and once he had seemed pretty big. Yes sir. For as I saw him smile, he seemed to shrivel down to less than a fraction of a man. Hunter couldn't change. He was still a born winner and could even rake in life's chips over the body of his dead son. Sometimes *it takes a long time and a particular set of circumstances to catch up with a man.*

I turned my horse as soon as I was able, moved Jake's head around to the east and thus turned my back on the scene. My eyes was fixed on the view to the east, so that it was like I wore blinders. I saw nothing else but the far horizon over towards the Panhandle where Lohman had come from. Everything else was blotted out. But I recollect saying to myself—"Now will they just leave him there?"

They left him all right. Behind me I could hear wagons creaking. I could hear horse movements. I could hear jingles and general movements. Some were a little slow in getting off and there was low-toned talk but they all moved out. When I turned around after I had made sure, and the only people left in the place were me and little Hank Harnish on his spotted pony who stayed like a kid would. I looked down and saw that I had Ferdy Maxwell's glasses slung on a strap on my chest. He'd just handed them to me when the Kid came out, and I'd forgotten all about that and about them until this minute. They had helped me see the sun on Tot's chest and the way his chest had seemed to suck the slugs in and the way he fell, but more than that they had showed me that he wasn't surrendering, nor thinking maybe they'd give him an hour or a day. He'd come to take it, because he wanted it.

I gave Henry a dollar and told him to ride his little pony in to Mel Parks, the undertaker, and get him out here in his spring wagon and to tell him if his own was busy he could ride over to my place and get our springer.

Henry disappeared and I rode Jake up as far as I could, then got off and led. I reached over and touched Lohman once, the back of his neck, where riding or walking ahead of me when we first met

*him near Clayton I had often sighted that tufted peak of hair grow-
ing down from his head. It was like a small boy's hair, like they call
it, a cowlick.*

*I walked over to the big rock he'd been using for cover. Never
thought at the time to look for his horse as it completely slipped my
mind. At the rear base of the rock was Lohman's rifle that would
not shoot again. He'd smashed it several times against the rock face,
so I could see the dim marks of the stock paint there.*

*Then I saw the shell that we thought was spent shell scattered
in front of the rock. The ones that had caught the light when he
throwed them over. They were not spent shell. They were live,
good cartridges. I think I got them all, counted them and stowed
them. . . .*

*Well, months have gone by and we're slowly getting over it. Nita
didn't speak to me for a long time and I dare say it will take her
even some more time to become resigned. To this day I don't realize
it. I don't think any of us do. Shucks, I know there are killings and
killings, for instance last week there was a sheepman torn to pieces
by something wild—nobody seems to know what—up by the north
Socorro hills. Word went all over. Then two months ago—maybe
three—a man was shot in the Muleshoe downtown. But come to
investigate—the sheepman he was a careless man who had been
warned about certain chances he was taking with the country he
was trying to get his stock to feed off. And the man at the saloon
was just a bum, got too big for his size and stopped Trouble the
wrong way.*

*But the point is you don't shoot up people like Lohman every
day, and it would not surprise me if something don't come of it.
There's still some talk of the federal people doing some investigating.*

I have developed quite a few busted friendships around and about. Am not too anxious to repair them. I saw to it that Mel did all right by Tot, and we put him in our plot where a Maxwell or two is buried and where nearly all of my wife's people are. A few days later somebody over on the west ridge found that little Blacky horse of Lohman's wandering around half starved with a broke leg and we had him shot. Then about two months later we went over to Socorro and dug up what was left of the old man and brought him and put him beside Tot. Seemed least we could do. As for his mother, we don't know where she lies, or the brothers. The living one, Harley, I guess was not much beans. Well, it's too bad. But it's a tough country, big and tough.

One thing sticks in my memory and keeps coming back about the Kid. Last time I saw him before he took death he was going up the stairs that last night. I was gabby-drunk and said something about, "Well, they gave you an awful chasing and you are still in trouble but you left your mark on them—"

Lohman wheeled, the only time he was ever downright angry with me. His blue eyes smoked up. He said: "Mr. Bradley, can't any people in the world understand that killing a man sickens a man?"

Night we buried the elder Lohman, Ferdy Maxwell came over with a cemetery paper for me to sign and we got to talking. Ferdy had had a few drinks and on a few he can get very mouthy and said he figured Lohman yellowed out toward the last. You understand that even sober all the brains Ferdy has he will do well to hang onto.

"Yellowed out?" I said. "Well, that is just plain foolishness." First, I told him it was not dead cartridges but live ones Tot threw away and then, realizing the lack of logic in that, I showed Ferdy the letter Tot left me the morning of the day he took permanent leave of us.

◆ ◆ ◆

Dear Mr. Bradley, Sir: Am getting out of this as do not wish to mix you up with me further. You have been kind enough. Thinking hard, seems to me Nelson was the only man I shot in cold blood, as have been crazy since, but am getting to see things in a fairer light. Also, Nelson rocked my horse so that he bled freely. My father used to say only a crazy man will keep on killing. Nelson will haunt me to my grave but I was crazy at the grove. If I ever kill a man again in a state of sound mind, I surely believe it will sour me against myself for good. This is not only my people's teaching but is normal.

I am pulled this way and that by what has happened to me and my people. I am like my brother, Nevin, trying to get a brace of mules to pull abreast when all their life they had pulled behind and afore. My father called—"Nevin, let go those hamestraps, you can't untrain a mule, they will pull you in two." So I say, shall I go to meet my people with more on my conscience? Or try to reach Wyoming? So the two mules pull me. I certainly will meet my people. All except Harley have preceded me and thus I feel like a lone stranger in a strange land. Ever your friend,

Tot Lohman.

ABOUT THE AUTHOR

Charles O. Locke (1896–1977) was an American author best known for his novels of the West. The scion of a newspaper family, he was born in Tiffin, Ohio, and graduated from Yale University. Locke began his career as a reporter at the *Toledo Blade* and before long moved to New York City, where he wrote for a number of newspapers, including the *New York Post* and the *New York World-Telegram*. Like many, he fell in love not only with the city but with its huge public library and access to the world of theater. He composed songs and libretti for stage shows, wrote plays for radio programs, and joined a local theater group, for which he wrote, directed, and performed, sometimes in his own plays.

Locke published his first novel, *A Shadow of Our Own*, in 1951, following it with his breakout success, *The Hell Bent Kid*, in 1957. The story of a young man in the 1880s who is unjustly pursued across the state of Texas by relentless enemies, this mesmerizing tale was heralded by the Western Writers of America as one of the top twenty-five Western novels of all time. 20th Century Fox adapted the book into a feature film, *From Hell to Texas*, in 1958.

The Southwest continued to fascinate Locke, and it provided the backdrop to two more, equally powerful novels, also set in the nineteenth century: *Amelia Rankin* (1959) and *The Taste of Infamy: The Adventure of John Killane* (1960).

CHARLES O. LOCKE

FROM OPEN ROAD MEDIA

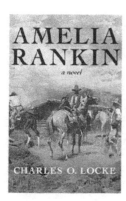

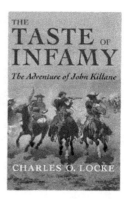

INTEGRATED MEDIA

Find a full list of our authors and
titles at www.openroadmedia.com

FOLLOW US
@OpenRoadMedia